MY GRANDFATHER

JACK the RIPPER

MY GRANDFATHER
JACK THE RIPPER

CLAUDIO APONE

HERODIAS

NEW YORK LONDON

Published by HERODIAS, INC.,
346 First Avenue, New York, NY 10009
HERODIAS, LTD., 24 Lacy Road, London, SW15 1NL
www.herodias.com

Manufactured in the United States of America

Design by Charles B. Hames
Jacket Art by Linda Paul
www.lindapaul.com

LIBRARY OF CONGRESS CATALOGING-IN-PUBLICATION DATA

Apone, Claudio 1961–
[Mio nonno Jack lo squartatore. English]
My grandfather Jack the Ripper / Cladio Apone.— 1st ed.
p. cm.
Summary: A clairvoyant thirteen-year-old uses his gifts to time travel
in search of clues to the unsolved crimes of Jack the Ripper,
but a more personal crime awaits him in the present.
ISBN 1-928746-16-0 (hb : alk. paper)
1. Jack the Ripper—Juvenile fiction. [1. Jack the Ripper—Fiction.
2. Boardinghouses—Fiction 3. Time travel—Fiction.
4. London (England)—Fiction. 5. England—Fiction.
6. Mystery and detective stories.] I. Title.
PZ7.A638 My 2000
[Fic]—dc21   00-044949

Originally published in Italian by La Spiga
Mio Nonno Jack Lo Squartatore
ISBN 88-468-1041-4

BRITISH LIBRARY CATALOGUING IN PUBLICATION DATA

A catalogue record of this book is available from the British Library

ISBN 1-928746-16-0

1 3 5 7 9 8 6 4 2

First edition 2001

MY GRANDFATHER

JACK THE RIPPER

CHAPTER

I

"Do you want to bet I can't guess what you have in your backpack for lunch?" says Andy Dobson, puffing out his chest with a smile and an air of challenge.

At that moment, the school bell starts clanging, calling to order the children who are waiting in the entrance hall, none of whom is in any hurry to go in.

"Let's go in now, and I'll guess afterwards."

Taking Lucy Catlett, his lifelong friend, by the hand, Andy runs toward their classroom. Though he has just turned thirteen years old, it seems to Andy that he has known Lucy forever. He is very fond of her and would do anything for her.

This unlikely pair is living proof of the theory that opposites attract. They are so different: She is scrupulous, meticulous, and extremely rational for her age. He is a loafer, a dreamer, untidy, and always ready to make fun of everything.

In spite of all this, the two are practically inseparable. Even so, their tender friendship often turns into a battle of wills every time one of them wants to convince the other of his way of thinking.

It should be pointed out that Lucy usually comes out on top, with her accusing finger forever pointed like some implacable judge from the Spanish Inquisition.

London is already cold and damp in October.

A dense, insidious fog envelopes everything, giving it a surreal look. Even sounds change. Everything's a bit more muffled, deadened, and . . . unsettling—because out of the fog something might suddenly emerge, something you would never want to see or experience.

While Lucy is taking off her overcoat and her long scarf, Andy takes her backpack and, gauging its weight, says in the solemn tone of a TV announcer, "Today . . . chocolate cake, buttered toast, and two fine apples . . . all wrapped up in a Harrod's shopping bag!"

"Don't pull that one on me! You've done it heaps of times already. Even so, I still don't know how you manage it," says Lucy.

Taking the Harrod's bag from her pink back-pack, she empties the contents onto her desk. Two lovely red apples roll out, followed by a large slice of chocolate cake and two, cellophane-wrapped slices of buttered toast.

Andy's happy laughter echoes around the classroom.

Andy has been aware of his gift ever since he was a toddler. Every time he holds something in his hands, something immediately and effortlessly takes shape inside his head—names, images. He is able to perceive a whole lot of things—for example, the history of the object and the person it belongs to. Andy has never taken this gift very seriously; mostly he uses it to amaze his friends.

He doesn't care to talk about it much for fear of being thought "different." Only Lucy and Andy's grandfather Bob know the whole story and, of course, his mum. She, however, never pays much attention to Andy and his gift; she is far too busy running the little East End boardinghouse owned by the Dobsons.

The East End is one of the poorest areas of London. Here the kids have to play football in the streets because they have nowhere else to go. Their parents are too busy trying to make ends meet to look after their children much.

The Jack-in-the-Box is a small dilapidated guest house located at No. 22 Batty Street not far from Whitechapel Road, right in the heart of the East End.

Through all its years, God only knows how many poor devils have slept, for a few pence, on tattered mattresses in those damp, shabbily furnished rooms.

Who knows how many weary, resigned legs have mounted those creaking wooden stairs in search of a bed on which to get some rest before facing another day filled with hardship.

Ah, yes! the Jack-in-the-Box may be a very poor-quality guest house, but it is chock-full of history. Nearly 150 years ago it was built by Andy's great-great-great-Grandfather Alistair Dobson; and from that day in 1853 when it opened, the Dobsons have been running it as best they can.

These days, it is Emma who manages things. Emma is Andy's mum, an attractive, authoritative young woman. One thing is sure—she isn't making a fortune. Things have gotten worse since the death of Andy's father, who died in a mysterious and tragic way when Andy was still very young.

Steve Dobson had been a Scotland Yard detective, much respected by his colleagues and by everyone who knew him. At the time of his death he was working undercover on a very important case, important enough to compel his killers to do away with him.

Andy remembers very little—he was only a few years old—but after coming across some newspaper articles his mum had carefully hidden, he learned, in the cruelest of ways, the details of his father's death.

The thing that Andy will never forget, however, was the look on his mum's face when his father's colleagues came to the Jack to report the finding of the body. It had been deathly cold in London that morning and a thin layer of frost had covered everything.

Steve Dobson's Rover, with him inside, had been dredged up from the bottom of the Thames. Subsequent investigations had gotten nowhere, and the case was filed away—but not in the hearts of Andy or his mum.

Granddad Bob is always around to lend Emma a hand. He is a big, burly, fine-looking man, full of energy despite his ninety-two years. He is inseparable from the pipe between his teeth and is fond of telling Andy terrifying legends and awful events that happened—or maybe never happened at all—a long time ago. Andy, for his part, is very attached to the old man and never tires of listening to him.

The little boardinghouse, with its five guest rooms—four, really, for room 4 has lain unused practically forever—is in need of a doing up. It could use a good coat of paint on the outside and a fair amount of work on the inside, especially on the wooden stairs that creak and groan like those in a haunted house.

On close inspection the boardinghouse does look a bit sinister, the exact opposite of the cheerful image that appears on the sign that hangs above the entrance: a painting of a jack-in-the-box. The idea of calling the boardinghouse by that name surely came from Alistair Dobson when he opened the place in 1853.

Today, the sign is somewhat rusty and dented—time corrodes all things. But surely this place must have known better days.

Alistair is remembered as a great kidder. When he wasn't too busy running the business, he would pass the time he could spare from his gin drinking by playing tricks and practical jokes on his friends and his lodgers. In other words, he was as mad as a March hare! The story is told of a dark night when, in order to get back at a guest who was in arrears with his rent, Alistair and his friends walled up the door of the man's room with bricks, causing him to nearly drop dead from fright in the morning.

Then there was another time when he served a pint of beer to a customer whom he didn't particularly like—after slipping a dead fish into the tankard!

This was how he earned the nickname "the Joker."

III

Granddad Bob is the true custodian of the Dobson family memories and he especially enjoys passing on everything he knows about his ancestors to his grandson, Andy. They often talk for hours and this usually drives Emma mad. She doesn't approve of having her son's head filled with a lot of rubbish.

As often happens, Andy has returned home from school and is having his tea in the kitchen in the company of Granddad Bob.

"Granddad, tell me more about the jokes that Alistair used to play."

"No Andy, your mum would give me a right telling off if she knew we were still talking about that stuff."

"Aw, come on, please . . . *please!*"

Andy knows Granddad will give in straight-away, as usual, because he, too, loves those old yarns.

"All right, then!" he says, lighting his pipe and settling himself comfortably in his chair, "but you mustn't think that the history of our family is all playing tricks and boozing. Lots of very strange things as well have happened over the years, and not all of them can be clearly explained. You see, we Dobsons are a special sort of folk. That goes for you, too, Andy, if we think of your strange gift—the gift that your mum doesn't want mentioned at any price. I believe in it, but don't tell her; I wouldn't put it past her to cut off my daily ration of gin, just to get back at me. . . .

"Anyway, I was saying . . . things started to go a bit wrong when William was born. That would be my grandfather—1858 I think it was, five years after the Jack-in-the-Box opened.

"William was born with a bad leg so he walked with a slight limp. In those days, you know, there weren't the treatments we have today, and, as a result, he grew up very sulky and closemouthed. Even as a boy he was always fighting and scrapping. Children used to goad him with the nickname, "the Gimp." He was a heartless little scoundrel.

"Alistair, his father, suffered so much on account of this that it even changed *his* personality. From being a cheerful practical joker, he turned surly and silent. They say that the lodgers could hear him sobbing in his room at night, if they listened hard. Things got even worse when William's mother, Margie, fell ill and died a couple of weeks later.

"Alistair found himself having to bring up the boy, who was only twelve at the time. It was no easy job, considering the lad's nasty disposition.

"The years that followed were pretty turbulent because, as he grew up, young William did nothing but get himself into trouble. He used to spend his nights chasing women or shooting dice, and he often rolled home drunk at dawn. He drank a lot, and there wasn't a day that he didn't get into a punch-up with other hotheads like himself.

"Soon after, Alistair, "the Joker," went to his reward and, barely eighteen then, William found himself with the responsibility of running the Jack-in-the-Box.

"Naturally, you can imagine that the quality of service at the guest house left a lot to be desired at the time; but, as fate would have it, William met Angela, a girl who, though not all that pretty, had her head screwed on right.

"It was from their marriage that Sonny, my father, was born in 1876. For the first few years William and Angela were happy; it even looked as if William had broken with his evil cohorts to devote himself more to the family and the business, which was showing some signs of improvement.

"But after those few happy years William went back to being his old self again: a surly, hard-drinking womaniser. And so everything went on amidst various ups and downs.

"Sonny grew bigger. He was an attractive child with gleaming reddish-blond curls and lively blue eyes.

"Everything went fine . . . until . . . the awful event."

"What awful event?" Andy breaks in with wide-eyed curiosity.

"It's not a story for children. Forget it."

But Andy won't be put off.

"If you don't tell me, I'll tell Mum that you pinch gin from the pantry!"

"Andy, it's not a story for a young boy's ears!"

The crafty little Andy starts yelling.

"Mumeee! I've got something to tell you . . . !"

Andy's grandfather, of course, gives in. He has no choice.

"Quiet . . . quiet, you little snake in the grass. I'll tell you!"

At that very moment Andy's mum, attracted by the yelling, comes into the kitchen.

She is perspiring heavily and carrying a big wicker basket full of freshly laundered clothes. From the look on her face, you can see that she is in no mood for jokes.

Though life has reserved many disappointments for her, and the work in the boardinghouse is very tiring, Emma, not yet thirty-five, still remains the beautiful woman she has always been.

And when she gets mad, she is even more beautiful.

Andy has inherited her tall, slim build, her impetuosity, her stubborn streak, and two spectacularly blue eyes you could see your reflection in.

"If you've finished with your meal, you can make yourselves useful by clearing the table and making less of a row—if you're able. I bet you've been telling the boy stories about your— What were you talking about, anyway? Ghosts wandering about the hotel? Headless women waving to passersby from the window or some such foolishness?"

She pauses briefly to get her breath. She has made herself hopping mad.

"Do the two of you want to see me dead?"

Bob stammers something incomprehensible, while Andy watches him with a sly grin on his face.

Then, all of a sudden, Emma turns on her heels and goes off upstairs.

As soon as they are alone, Andy urges Granddad to go on with the story.

"All right, all right, then. . . . Well, in the winter of 1888, early November, it was—in room four there lived a girl from Wales, she was, a certain Mary Jane, who, later on . . ."

"Who later on what?" insists Andy, who is getting more and more impatient.

"Who . . . nothing at all!" says Granddad curtly. "She died, and that was it!"

Andy, bursting with curiosity, starts tugging at the poor man's shirt.

"Granddad! Don't be so mysterious, *please*!"

For the hundredth time, Granddad gives in.

"Well, all right then. She was a pretty girl, was Mary Jane, and she had lots of friends who used to give her presents on account of how kind she was to them. That's how she made her living."

Andy breaks into a loud laugh.

"I understand, Granddad! Sort of like Miss Carla Cooper!"

Miss Cooper is a lodger in the guest house—a beautiful Jamaican woman who says she is a hostess for British Airways

When she came to London, with just a few pounds in her pocket, she took up residence in the Jack-in-the-Box because it had at once struck her as being cheaper than other places. Besides, she had gotten on well with Andy right from the start, and immediately a bond of friendship was formed. At heart, she is still a little girl. She is very kind as well; whenever she comes back from Kingston, in Jamaica, where her parents live, she never fails to bring along little presents—two bottles of rum for Granddad Bob and some CDs of reggae music for Andy.

Carla Cooper is not only nice and kind. She is also one of those women you can't help noticing when they pass by—her full lips and her feline walk, almost as if she were a fashion model, never pass unnoticed; and she frequently gets admiring comments from men who are lucky enough to meet her.

Thanks to her statuesque figure, she has an army of admirers who come to call on her in her room at all hours and do loads of favours for her, like paying her rent and settling her bills in the shops she frequents.

Anyway, Andy nearly splits his sides laughing to see how embarrassed Granddad had suddenly become.

"Come on, Granddad, don't make such a face! These days, kids my age know a lot more than you think. I know exactly what Miss Cooper gets up to. One night, when I couldn't sleep, I counted four or five men coming out of Miss Cooper's room, and there were all sorts of noises coming from the room as well."

Overcoming his embarrassment with some difficulty, Granddad resumes his story.

"All right, then! Poor Mary Jane did the same kind of work. Of course, it's not a very honourable profession; but in those days, there was more poverty in the East End than you can ever imagine and so lots of folks had to do as best they could. Anyhow, one morning—"

At that instant, Emma comes back into the kitchen. When she sees them still sitting there, she really blows her top.

After giving Bob another telling off, she gives Andy a sound kick on the backside and sends him off to study in his room.

IV

With his hands pressed to his aching behind, Andy scampers along the corridor separating the kitchen from his little bedroom.

The huge, stuffed heads of stags and wild boars adorning the dark wooden walls seem to be scrutinising his every move in the shadowy gloom.

I wonder why Mum never opens the windows in this corridor? Andy thinks.

He has never liked all those animals hanging up there on the wall. Quite the opposite. Ever since he was a small child he had taken to walking down the corridor at a fast pace, almost as if he were afraid that one of them might come down off the wall and grab him.

But that is only part of it. The dining room is even worse. Among the big, battered wooden tables lay a scattering of goatskins and a zebra hide, trophies from some big game safari. Around

the dented fender of the fireplace is the prize
specimen: a magnificent tiger skin covered with
grease stains and cigarette burns.

Its gaping jaws are probably home to a family
of spiders—and who can tell where one of its
glass eyes has ended up? All in all, the tiger
makes Andy feel kind of sorry for him—a far cry
from his cousins who, even now, are padding
about in some jungle or other, looking very
pleased with themselves. Oh, man! Think of the
look on their faces if they could see him now!

In the middle of the muddle of funereal bad
taste—smelling of rotten wood—Andy's room is
the only one that looks passable.

When you go in, it doesn't look as if you are
inside the guest house at all. A large window
sheds light on the walls, which are completely
covered with posters, with Oasis and U2 standing
out above the rest. Scattered all around the desk
next to his computer lies a confused jumble of
schoolbooks and comics—Japanese Manga,
mostly. Andy is crazy about Manga.

Suspended here, there, and everywhere are
those small, evergreen-scented deodourising
trees. They were a gift from Lucy, who

maintained that they did a good job of covering up the smell of damp towels and rotten wood that characterises the dilapidated structure.

In the whole house, Andy's room is the only place that is worth living in. Everywhere else gives him a feeling of heavy oppression.

While he is surfing the Net to pass the time, Lucy comes in, as usual.

"What are studying now, eh?" Lucy wants to make it clear that she knows very well how inclined he is to idle away his time.

Andy doesn't even bother to reply. Instead, he starts telling her what Granddad told him and imagines what he *would* have told him if his mum hadn't interrupted them just when the story was getting good.

Unlike Andy, Lucy doesn't care much for all those mysterious stories about the past that her friend is so fond of; on the contrary, more than once she had informed him in no uncertain terms that the stories scared her. So Andy, who is every bit as much a teaser as his ancestor Alistair, "the Joker," enjoys telling her taller and taller tales just to terrify her. To tell the truth, this is a crafty move on his part, because sometimes when Lucy gets frightened she looks for comfort in his arms and hugs him close—something he doesn't object to at all . . . not in the slightest!

They went on with these little games for some time, doing a little bit of everything except, naturally, what Lucy came to do every day: homework.

But, all of a sudden, something happens that catches their attention: an odd noise seems to be coming from behind the door to Andy's room. The two children look at one another.

Poor Lucy is suddenly pale.

It sounds exactly as if some huge beast is scratching its back against the door.

"You and all your weird stories," says Lucy in a shaking voice. "I want to go home and—and I don't ever want to come back to this nut house again!"

Straining his ears, Andy walks towards the door.

The sound of scratching and heavy breathing is coming from the other side. He plucks up his courage and flings open the door.

The sight that meet his eyes is, to say the least, unusual: the panting animal is none other than Miss Carla Cooper the "hostess."

Standing there at the door, barefoot and wearing a slip that is almost the same colour as her skin, she is holding two cups of steaming hot chocolate in her hands. She tries to say something but can't speak until Andy takes the packet of biscuits she is holding between her teeth.

Carla gets her breath back and lets out a long sigh. "Pheeeew! . . . hard to open the door carrying all this stuff. Hi, kids! I heard you coming in so I made some hot chocolate for you."

The two youngsters gape at Carla in her slip in utter surprise for a few seconds.

"What tense faces! I'll go away if I'm bothering you!"

"No! No!" replies Andy. "It's just that, well, y'know . . . Forget it. It's too silly."

Carla is always very nice, obliging, and ready to help everyone—always very considerate with Andy and Lucy. Her only fault, if you could call it a fault, is that when she starts talking, she never stops. She sounds like machine gun gone haywire.

In a few minutes she has repeated the story of her life. Then she starts in about her latest flight, London to Capetown, explaining how her feet get all swollen from running up and down the plane handing out drinks and newspapers to rude, bad-tempered passengers.

Then she talks about air pockets and turbulence—how she hasn't yet gotten used to them and how it upsets her during the flights, to see passengers puking and crying with fright at the same time.

At the end of all this, she shows the two children, by now drunk on words, a lovely ring which, she says, was given to her by a suitor.

She is interrupted by Lucy, who was now fed up to the teeth, just as Carla was about to start in on another of her favourite topics.

"Look, Carla, we could sit here for hours listening to you, but we've got to study a little. . . ."

Carla, who is anything but stupid, catches on straightaway.

"Okay . . . okay. I'll go listen to some music in my room," she says, grabbing a Red Hot Chili Peppers CD from Andy's desk. "I'll bring it back later!"

With that she leaves the room with a distinct twirl of her hips, leaving the empty cups and the biscuits behind.

"This is really a nuthouse!" repeats Lucy as soon as they are alone.

"Does it strike you as normal that this Cooper woman wanders round the hotel half naked?"

"You wouldn't be jealous by any chance?" Andy asks, giving her a sidelong glance.

"You've got to be kidding! If you ask me, she's pure silicon."

"No, no. She's a hundred percent natural."

"And how would you know?"

"She told me so herself. . . . Why, what were you thinking?" replies Andy, chuckling ambiguously. "Anyhow," he goes on as a curious sort of grin lights up his face, "you ain't seen nothin' yet."

"In the room next to Carla's right now—in Room one—there's a young man—he's just arrived. A very funny sort of bloke. Never talks, never says hello to anyone and, if you ask me, he never sleeps."

"How do you know?" said Lucy.

"Often, when I stay up late at night on the Net, I happen to go to the kitchen for a glass of milk.

Every time I pass his room I see a light under his door . . . at all hours."

"Then I'm right to think that this is a nut-house," says Lucy. "Your friend Carla is out of her mind. And now you tell me about a bloke who never talks to anyone and who never sleeps. All we need is a mad scientist and then—"

"Yes! Yes! that's it," Andy breaks in, "you nearly got it right. We've got one of them, too. . . . Dr. Whitmore—he's been here for ages, and he's got a thing for chemistry. I peeped into his room once.

"He's installed a lab bench in there at least three metres long. He spends the whole day hunched over that table, which is loaded with retorts, and test tubes, and other diabolical stuff. He does strange experiments and won't talk about them. As you can imagine, my mum would like to get rid of him because she's afraid he'll blow us all up one day."

"That makes three." says Lucy with a touch of resignation in her voice. "Who's the fourth nutter, the creature from the Black Lagoon?"

"Don't know, Lucy. The fourth is a high-class old gent who came here a couple of days ago from

Devonshire. I've only seen him a few times, but he looks like an ordinary person."

"Then he won't be staying long, if he's that normal. . . ."

"Oh! I'm forgetting." Andy goes on, jumping up from the armchair. "We've got room four, the one I often talk to you about—now that's the real mystery—locked up, untouched for years and years and woe betide anyone in the family who mentions it. Just think, even Granddad only remembers it as being closed, so you can imagine how long it's been since anyone went in there."

"I bet," says Lucy, "that you're just dying to poke around in there!" Her tone was midway between provocative and the quarrelsome.

"Good for you! You're a really brainy little kid. You're right. One of these days I'll get hold of the key and go have a look. Before my mum interrupted us at tea today, Granddad was telling me about something that happened here long ago. I reckon it had to do with room four."

It was at times like this that Lucy thinks Andy is really irresponsible, and she trembles at the thought of what sort of trouble he is likely to get himself into. But she is very fond of him and would follow him to the ends of the earth—because Andy is kind of her knight in shining armour.

Once, at school, the Daniels brothers, Roddy and Martin, were pestering her and Andy arrived to sort things out. What a punch-up! From that day on, the Daniels boys have greeted her with great respect.

V

Evening came. As usual, Andy and Lucy didn't study a whole lot.

Back at the Jack-in-the-Box after walking Lucy home, Andy hangs around in reception, playing with the cat to pass the time until supper.

The reception counter snakes the length of the hall like a long, dead earthworm. The dust-covered guest book lies there, always open to the same page. It is never used anyway.

There hasn't been a desk clerk there for years; maybe there had never been one. It costs too much to pay a security staff, and, anyhow, Emma says that the portrait of old Alistair that hangs on the wall, with his wild expression—half clown, half devil—is worth more than a whole pack of ferocious guard dogs.

After supper is finished, eaten as usual in the company of Granddad, Emma sends Andy to serve the evening meal, as ordered, to the occupant of room 1.

This is the sort of chore that usually gets on Andy's nerves, lazy as he is; but this time he accepts with good grace because he is curious to meet this new, unsociable guest.

He hurries along the corridor—the one he doesn't like at all—holding the tray in his hands, careful not to upset anything. When he gets to the door, he knocks on it with a couple of kicks of his foot. After waiting in vain for a reply, he decides to open it using his elbow—a manoeuvre worthy of one of those contortionists you see at a circus.

Warily, he enters the gloom.

A handkerchief draped over the lamp creates a glowing, surreal atmosphere. Almost feeling his way, and being extra careful not to fall over, tray and all—he advances further into the room, where a young man, all curled up into a ball like a cat, seems to be sleeping; although the sound of music can be heard coming from the earphones of the Walkman he is wearing.

Up to that time, Andy had thought that he held the unenviable title of the World's Untidiest

Boy; but after glancing around the room, he realises that he'll have to rethink that one.

"I wish my mum could see this room now," he mutters, looking for an empty space on which to set the tray.

The desk is covered in books, some of which are open. Other books are in piles all over the place. Here and there, empty cigarette packets, underwear thrown carelessly onto the floor, and the remains of some McDonald's meals reign supreme. Also, the air that Andy breathes isn't any better than the look of the room. From the smell of smoke and dirty socks, he can tell that the mysterious young man doesn't worry too much about airing the place.

While he is setting down the tray in the only space free of paper and food scraps, Andy rattles the crockery with an awkward jolt. The young man twitches and turns on his side so that the amateur waiter is able to get a look at his face. The man opens his eyes one at a time, as if he wants to be sure he is where he thinks he is.

"Where did you spring from?" he mumbles, pulling the headphones from his ears.

"My name is Andy Dobson and this is your supper" he replies, a little grouchily.

Seen standing up, now that he has gotten out of bed, the young man looks much taller than he had seemed lying down: his short hair and his youthful face give him an honest, reassuring, though somewhat diffident quality.

"You're not from around here?" Andy queries, just to break the ice.

"Is my English still that awful, even though I've been in London quite a while now? Great!" he says with an amused smile. "Well, anyway you're right, I'm Italian."

"You a student?"

"Yes, English literature and history."

"I hope you like the food, 'cuz my mum cooked it."

"Ah! Your mum is the cook?"

"That's right. Cook, charwoman, washer-woman, waitress, and the owner of the hotel as well."

"Hotel?" said the young man with an amused smile. "To me it looks like a cross between a museum and the house of horrors!"

"If you don't like it here you can go away," Andy says, feeling a bit insulted.

The young man, realising he has put his foot in it, apologises to the part-time waiter and asks him to please take a seat. Andy, who is still on his guard, nevertheless finds him friendly enough; he drops into an armchair after removing the suit-case that was occupying it.

"Look, I decided to take lodgings here with you for a couple of reasons. First of all, it's cheap; second, it has to do with my research. As a matter of fact, I'm preparing my finals and this neighbourhood and the Jack are of historical signi-ficance for my thesis."

Andy is already spellbound by the young man with the strange accent—but even more so by the subject of his studies. Massimo, that's what the young man says his name is—says he comes from Milan.

As Massimo wolfs down the frugal supper— some fried chicken wings with broccoli on the side—he becomes the target of a volley of questions directed at him by Andy, who is becoming more and more curious.

"Why are you so interested in what I'm doing?" asks Massimo.

"I love these old stories, especially the ones that talk about this boardinghouse and this neighbourhood. My granddad Bob tells me lots of them and I can listen to him for hours."

"Then you probably know," the young Italian goes on, "that this area has always been very poor and, of course, one hundred—one hundred fifty years ago, it certainly didn't look the way it looks now."

"So how did it look?" asks Andy, settling himself comfortably into the armchair.

"Try to picture a flood of ragged men, women, and children wandering about in alleyways choked with garbage; unhealthy damp houses infested with rats and beetles; poverty and disease; vice and degradation. At that time, there were at least a million people living in the East End—unemployed, outcasts of society, criminals, wretches who would turn to anything just to survive. There! survival—that was the main problem, a pitiful day-to-day struggle.

"As for my thesis, I'm trying to reconstruct the history of the East End at the end of the nineteenth century, with special regard to certain 'foul deeds' that took place and other things as well."

This was already the second time that day that someone—first Granddad and now Massimo—had aroused Andy's curiosity with stories of "foul deeds" only to leave him unsatisfied.

"What 'foul deeds'?"

"I don't think it's a story for someone your age."

Andy breaks in resentfully, "I'm not a baby anymore, and anyhow I could tell you loads of things you would never find in any of your damn books! For instance, all the things that Granddad knows about all our ancestors; things he tells only to me."

"So, you'd be a Dobson then?" Massimo asks with interest.

"Yeah. You said it!" replies Andy scornfully

Then he begins talking about old Alistair, "the Joker"; William "the Gimp"; and about all the old stories that Granddad Bob entertains him with in front of dining room fireplace on long winter evenings.

Andy is proud to be a Dobson, and you can tell this from the feeling he puts into his telling about the old tales. For his part, Massimo listens silently until Andy makes a passing reference to his strange and mysterious gift. It is at this point that the Italian student bursts into a roar of laughter.

"And here I am wasting my time with a kid! Cut it out! I don't believe it. You?"

Andy is furious. If there is one thing he can't stand, it is for someone to start casting doubts on what he says.

"Want me to show you?"

"Okay," replies Massimo. "Let's have a bit of fun, I really need that. I've been cooped up here studying for three days, not putting a foot outside the door. Let's hear your story."

As he says this, from around his neck he takes a gold chain bearing a lucky charm set with blue stones.

Andy takes the piece of jewelry in his hands and begins passing it from one hand to the other. Then he half closes his eyes beneath Massimo's semiserious gaze and begins talking very slowly.

"It's a gift from a girl."

"It's not that hard if you go by guesswork," says Massimo ironically.

"And your girl suffers a lot from the fact that you don't see each other very often. She loves you very much."

"Yeah! Well you don't need second sight for that, seeing as I'm over here and she's in Italy. These are tricks you can learn from a magician on a TV show. Even so, you've got some talent," he goes on, still teasing him without taking him too seriously.

But as soon as Andy starts describing the girl physically, in great detail, Massimo stops smirking and his face becomes serious and pale.

"What's more," Andy continues, "at this very minute she's in pain on account of something wrong with her leg—maybe a fall."

When he hears this, Massimo is so upset and astonished that his eyes nearly pop out of his head.

Andy has just given such an exact description of places and faces, that Massimo's skepticism is transformed into an explosion of amazement that makes him leap up from his seat.

"Yes! yes! It's true! Donatella phoned me the other day. She's broken her ankle skiing! But Andy does your mum know you have these . . . these powers?"

"Oh, yes! But she's always telling me not to talk about them to anyone, 'cuz people might think I was a bit soft in the head."

CHAPTER

VI

"Andy, listen to me carefully. Has anyone ever talked to you about psychometry?"

"Uh-huh," the boy replies. "Ever since I was a kid I was aware of this strange thing. For instance, I always knew what was in the Christmas gifts before I unwrapped them. It's kind of hard to describe the sensation, but it's very distinct. There are objects that have no effect on me at all, while, if I handle others, it's as if they start to tell me their life stories whether I want them to or not. It's like a little man is inside my head who starts to analyse what I'm holding in my hand and tells me everything. I've gotten used to it now, but at the beginning it used to scare me. By the way, it doesn't happen only with objects but with places, too."

"But haven't you ever spoken to an expert?" inquires Massimo, who is more than ever convinced that he is in the presence of something quite out of the ordinary.

"No, never. Well, not really . . . When I was ten I went on a school trip to Scotland, and we did the usual tour—castles, ancient buildings, and museums. Inside one of those museums, an old building a few miles from Edinburgh, when I went into the last room, I started to feel a sensation of great heat but I didn't pay much attention at first. Soon after, my nostrils started burning like when you sniff boiling hot tea, and, in the end, I began to choke."

"And then?" Massimo demands eagerly, becoming more and more mesmerised by Andy's story.

"Well, as you can probably imagine, I felt terrible, and, what's more, a whole bundle of sensations started overlapping one another.

I became aware of an acrid burning smell, and I found myself gasping for breath. I looked around at my mates, but it seemed that I was the only person to sense the odour. Then I had to sit down—I was that weak. And then the teacher came—worried stiff she was—asking me how I was feeling. I felt faint already, on account of the smoke that only I could smell and I started to hear the sound of people running, the panicky trampling of lots of people . . . and screams.

"Then the teacher said, 'Get him outside. Let him have some air!'

"They stretched me out in the garden, and in a couple of minutes I started breathing normally again. The sensation of heat went away, and I couldn't hear the sound of people running or the screams anymore.

"On the way home the teacher bombarded me with questions. I still remember the way her eyes bulged when I gave her a detailed description of the sensations I had felt. But even then, I was really frightened. I was scared that I was sick, but I never thought of those special gifts until . . ."

"Until? Go on, Andy! This is fascinating."

"Until a few days after we had got back from the trip, the teacher came to the boardinghouse, accompanied by a real professor-type guy, who she said was a special kind of doctor. This character, very serious looking, asked me loads of questions—like had I ever been to Edinburgh before and had I ever had experiences like this before.

"Soon after asking me all these questions, he told us a story that, for the moment, left us feeling shocked and amazed.

"He told us that fifty years before, just after the war, the museum had been a school that was also used as a summer camp for about two hundred young boys and girls. On one summer's night, maybe because of a electrical short circuit, a raging fire broke out. Some of the young campers got out of the building straightaway, but a large number of them, especially the younger ones, were trapped. Threatened by the smoke and flames, they retreated all the way to the farthest room in an attempt to save themselves—the very room where I had felt sick. They tried to get out through the windows, but the iron grilles prevented them.

"It was a terrible tragedy because every one of them died, suffocated by the smoke. After the fire was put out, the rescuers found themselves faced with a scene straight out of one of those cult suicides: more than eighty children piled up on top of one another on the floor. The littler ones were clinging to the older ones to find courage and that's how they were found—in an embrace of death."

Massimo, speechless in the face of such a tragedy, gestures at Andy to go on.

"It was then that I understood what had happened. Inside that school I had relived that tragic night. I travelled the same path as those poor little children . . . experienced what they had experienced. I could feel their terror and . . . in effect, they died all over again and I died with them. I must admit I was quite scared when I heard those explanations, even though, by then, I'd gotten used to such things."

"But then . . ." Massimo inquired, surprised by the mature way in which Andy expressed himself, "that strange doctor with the teacher, what did he want exactly?"

"Ha! ha! ha! That's when my mum blew her top and threw them both out of the house."

"Why on earth . . . ?"

"Because they wanted to take me to some kind of clinic in Sussex that specialised in that sort of thing, where they would stick me full of electrodes and carry out a whole raft of tests . . . encephalograms and stuff like that.

"You should have heard my mum screaming: 'My son's not going to be a guinea pig in your experiments! He's not a monster!' So off they went and we never saw them again.

"That day, my mum told me never to breathe a word to anyone about what had happened and that she never wanted to mention the subject again for any reason whatsoever."

"It's all so extraordinary," replies Massimo, "but I don't understand what your mother was afraid of—as if she were in the presence of witchcraft. On the contrary, it's a very special cognitive phenomenon known as psychometry, when the subject—in this case, you—is placed in contact with an object, he perceives its history and everything that has happened to it."

"Mum does it for my own good. She wants to protect me. She's afraid that this thing might create complexes in me and that people will make malicious gossip about it, encouraged by the fact that there are already nasty stories floating around concerning the Jack-in-the-Box boardinghouse."

At least a quarter hour went by before the young Italian student had recovered from the shock of the story he had just been told.

Meanwhile, Andy had strutted out the room, proud as a peacock at having put an end to Massimo's teasing and condescending smiles.

VII

In a short while, Andy returns to Massimo's room to find the student staring blankly out the window.

"Now that I've shown you what I can do, how about telling me some stories about the old East End?"

And Massimo, lighting his umpteenth cigarette, again takes up the tale. "Well, you see, in those days, as I mentioned already, there was a lot of poverty and people were prepared to do any kind of work, turn their hand to anything, just to survive. Folks got by doing a little stealing here and there, and there were many women who, just to scrape together enough money to feed their children, went around entertaining men who rewarded them for their company with two or three pence.

"You realise what sort of a charming little environment it was? Around here, at the end of the nineteenth century, it was pure chaos. Disease was everywhere—lots of children never reached the age of three because, long before that, they got sick and died."

Andy's face grows suddenly dark. He is struck by the story with its atmosphere of catastrophe, and he thinks sadly of all those unfortunate people.

"Poor great-great-grandfather William—life couldn't have been very easy for him."

"No," says Massimo, "life wasn't easy for any-one in the East End in those days. Then, as if all that weren't enough, somebody started killing people—certain women—in a horrible manner."

Andy's curiosity is at its height, and so, burst-ing with impatience, he urges Massimo to go on with the story.

"You see," says Massimo, consenting to his wish, "between August 31 and November 9, 1888, somebody, whose identity remains a mystery to this day, murdered five poor young women from this area using the most indescribably atrocious methods—all women of the kind I have just been telling you about."

"You mean the sort of women who get men to pay them?"

"Precisely," Massimo goes on. "All this happened in these alleyways near Whitechapel Road—here in Batty Street, next to this boardinghouse. What's more—now don't get scared—the last crime, the one on November 9, took place right here, in one of the rooms of the Jack-in-the-Box. Andy, did you *never* hear of Jack the Ripper?"

Young Andy Dobson is at a fever pitch of excitement. All at once lots of things seem to become clear to him. So that is why he had all those strange sensations during his childhood here at the Jack-in-the-Box!

That explains the strange feeling he gets when he goes along the corridor and past certain rooms . . . and all those sleepless nights made restless by monstrous thoughts that seem to come to him from out of nowhere. And it is even worse when he does manage to fall asleep. Then, after crossing the "dark threshold" (that was the nickname he had given it), he finds himself catapulted into a foggy, ice-cold universe made up of foul-smelling alleyways. The smell is so sickening that, sometimes, when he wakes up in the morning, it seems to him that the odour has impregnated his clothes. There's more: a recurring dream—one where coaches drawn by black horses suddenly come hurtling out of nowhere and, after trying to run him down, disappear around a corner.

Of course! Now it is clear. These strange feelings are the result of his special sensitivity and not just the imaginings of a distracted schoolboy. So, something dreadful that in some way involves him has happened within these walls. Someone or *something* is trying to contact him or—or at least, that is the feeling he has.

Who knows how many dreadful events these dilapidated walls have witnessed? Who knows how many sinister conversations the crude, rickety wooden tables in the dining room must have overheard? And all those revolting, stuffed animals that populate the corridors—what atrocities have their cold, glassy eyes observed?

Ah! if only those objects, these walls, this furniture could speak. For anyone else, any attempt to question inanimate objects would be out of the question. But for him, Andy Dobson, a descendant of Alistair, "the Joker," and William, "the Gimp," all this represents anything but an impossible problem. On the contrary, it only serves to strengthen Andy's conviction that his gifts were not given to him by chance but in accordance with some precise, superior plan.

Andy is more than ever certain that, independent of his will, he is destined for a mission from which there is no escape: to rip aside the dark, ponderous veil covering the atrocious, unsolved mysteries of the past. He is becoming more and more convinced that this mission will never end—a restless, aimless journey across a wasteland of black ice ceaselessly lashed by winds of unimaginable force, where neither time nor memory exist. A mission to a place where demons drip with blood, with poverty and degradation, freezing houses, distraught mothers—where enormous rats emerge from the sewers to bite poor, newborn babies in their cradles. It is now up to him, like a knight in a medieval saga, to challenge the darkness and to defeat it.

Andy Dobson.

Is that the reason why his mum and granddad Bob never want to talk about certain subjects? Do they know?

VIII

Just as all these thoughts are jostling and shoving one another in his brain like a crowd milling about in the Underground, a flash of insight strikes Andy like a shot from a gun.

"Room four!"

His voice bursts from his throat with such force that Massimo nearly has a heart attack.

Andy paces up and down the room like a tiger in a cage, ignoring the Italian student's repeated pleas for him to remain calm. At a certain point, there is nothing left for Massimo to do but lift Andy up bodily and dump him like a sack of potatoes in the armchair.

"At last, Andy! You look like someone possessed. You really have me scared. Maybe I was wrong to tell you certain things."

Andy seems to be calmer now and, after sipping some tea left over from Massimo's supper, by now stone-cold, is encouraged to talk about room 4.

"Granddad told me about Room four on the first floor. It's been locked up for so many years that even he doesn't remember how long. . . . He told me that in his grandfather William's day it was occupied by a young woman who came to a bad end—she died—a certain Mary Jane."

"Yes! yes! That's it! Mary Jane Kelly, the fifth victim, the one killed on November 9, 1888."

Now their roles seem to have been switched.

Compared to Andy, who appears to have calmed down, Massimo, at the mention of Mary Jane and of her room, has become very excited.

"Do you mean to tell me that the room on the first floor belonged to Mary Jane and has been shut up from that day and that nobody has ever set foot in it since?"

Andy confirms this several times and, by common agreement, they very daringly decide that it is essential to go and have a look as soon as possible.

"But now, let's talk about this Mary Jane," says Andy.

"Okay." Massimo begins to tell the story. "This Kelly woman was born in Limerick, Ireland, but when she was very young she moved with her family to Wales, where her father worked as a coal miner. At the age of sixteen she married a man who was also a miner. When her husband died in a mine accident a couple of years later, she moved to Cardiff. It couldn't have been easy for a woman, and a widow at that, to survive in those days; maybe that's why she turned to prostitution.

"In 1884 she arrived in London, where at first she stayed in a convent in which she earned her bed and board by doing chores like cooking and cleaning. Later on, it seems, she started to work in a brothel for rich gentlemen in the West End."

"Bloody hell!" Andy exclaims. "It must have been really tough living in those days. But what sort of woman was this Mary Jane?"

"Well, as far as I can make out, it seems that poor Mary Jane Kelly was a pretty woman—blond hair, blue eyes, a bit stout, but with all the right things in all the right places. They say she was very friendly, except when she'd had one too many. Then, it seems, she used to get a bit rowdy."

"In other words,"—laughs Andy "—a bit like Granddad Bob. When he gets tight he makes an awful row—staggering about, singing at the top of his voice—until my mum gets real mad and sends him off to bed."

"Exactly." Massimo continues, "Anyhow, apart from this, she was a quiet girl, well liked by all. At the time of her death she was about twenty-five years old, and the last time she was seen that night, she was wearing a red shawl. What's more, she must have been very fond of singing because, afterwards, her neighbours testified that they heard her singing in her room for hours before the murder."

"And what was she singing?" Andy demands.

"Who cares, for Pete's sake!" Massimo bursts out, annoyed at so much curiosity.

"*I* care, that's who. I care a lot! If we're going to be an effective team of detectives you've got tell me absolutely everything you know . . . also, because neither Mum nor Granddad have ever told me anything about this. . . ."

Resigned and somewhat irritated by the boy's insistence, Massimo goes on.

"It appears she always used to sing the same tune: an old folk song, a sad, nostalgic lament, something, as I recall, involving mothers and death—childhood memories and flowers plucked from graves. I think it was called . . . umm . . . 'A Violet from Mother's Grave.'"

"Would you like to sing it to me?" Andy interrupts him in mocking tones.

"If you think I'm going to start singing into the bargain, you're making a big mistake . . . and anyway, it's time you left."

"Okay. If you don't want me to know anything more about that little ditty . . . pity, I was curious."

Then Massimo, perhaps regretting that he has been rude to the boy, takes a book from one of the large bags on the floor of the room and starts to read:

"Scenes of my childhood arise before my gaze,
Bringing recollections of bygone happy days.
When down in the meadow in childhood I
*   would roam*
No one's left to cheer me now within that good
*   old home.*
Father and Mother, they have pass'd away,
Sister and brother, now lay beneath the clay,

*But while life does remain to cheer me, I'll
    retain
This small violet I plucked from my Mother's
    grave.*

"That's the text of the song—happy now?" says Massimo, replacing the book.

"Yes, but there's one last thing I want to ask you: What were you listening to on your Walkman?"

"Paganini. *Twenty-four Caprices*. Ever hear of it?"

"No . . ." replies Andy with a shrug of this shoulders. "Better than Britney Spears?"

"What does she have to do with Paganini!" Massimo snorts, horrified at the comparison. "Nicolò Paganini was the greatest violinist of all time—a total genius—and anyhow, he lived more than a century ago."

"He was an Italian too. I imagine."

"He sure was," Massimo replies with pride. "What's more, the best violin makers were, and still are, Italians: Amati, Stradivari, Guarneri del Gesù—and it's now certain that the first violin was made in Italy in 1500."

"The only Italian musicians I know are 883—they cut a track with BoyZone here in London not long ago."

"I know them too," Massimo replies—Max Pezzali and 883. But that's popular stuff; Paganini is classical. But what's the point? You will have to listen to him to understand. It's my belief that the sound of the violin has therapeutic powers. When I get home after one of those days when everything goes wrong, I just fall into an armchair, close my eyes, and let myself be carried away by its sound. . . . Soon I start to feel completely detached from all the things I thought were so important during the day—the things that stressed me out disappear as if by magic. It's a state of abandonment that's so sweet and so special that I can hardly put it into words . . ."

"Wow!" says Andy, impressed by the vehemence with which Massimo is describing his feelings. "They really do get to you, those violins!"

"Sure. I don't think any other instrument can interpret our states of mind better than the violin. There's life and death in its sound, laughter and tears . . . the same irrepressible power that there is in poetry and storytelling. The violin is not just an inanimate object; it tells you something because it has a life of its own—it's alive! You have to listen to understand. . . ."

Twenty-four Caprices is one of my favourites, and the solo violin on the recording is an authentic Stradivarius. If you promise to leave now, I'll lend it to you."

"Ah . . . you'll *lend* it to me?"

Andy, most of the time, finds a special joy in doing the opposite of what others expect him to do. In this case, he understands that Massimo just wants him to go, so he does the opposite.

"If you get lost, I'll *give* you the CD," says Massimo limply.

Before taking leave of each other—for it is nearly midnight by now—they make a solemn vow not to speak to anyone of the adventure they are about to undertake.

Grabbing the Paganini CD, Andy thanks Massimo and vanishes swiftly from the room. As soon as he enters his room, Andy locks the door. That way he feels safer.

That night, they both sleep very little, and the little sleep they do get is restless. Massimo, reflecting on Andy's psychic powers, plans to make use of them. *Andy could be useful to me in shedding some light on the whole Ripper affair,* he thinks.

Andy's short sleep, on the contrary, is filled with dreams of men in top hats and black cloaks, who peer at him from around dark corners and rooms whose floors are littered with parts of human bodies and whose walls are spattered with blood right up to the ceiling. Towards daybreak he has the recurrent dream: the one about the horse-drawn carriage that hurtles out of the darkness and tries to run him down.

IX

The next morning, Andy gets up more tired than he was before he had gone to bed. He would gladly have foregone his morning lessons, but since he had used up his entire range of excuses—from bellyache, to backache, to headache—he knew that his mum wouldn't swallow the story. She would kick his butt all the way to his classroom. So he didn't even try. With his heart filled with melancholy, he set off towards school.

Harry Catlett of the London Metropolitan Police is not only the local bobby in Whitechapel Road and the surrounding area, but also he happens to be the father of Lucy, the only person Andy will listen to. Harry is like Andy's conscience, always ready to point an accusing finger at him like a pistol, always telling him what he ought and ought not to do.

The very last person he wants to meet is P.C. Catlett, always so generous with his reprimands and advice. At corner of Burslem Street and Cannon Street, two blocks away from the council school, the policeman appears accompanying his daughter to her classes.

"Hello, Mr. Catlett. Nice day today, isn't it?"

"It sure doesn't look like a nice day to me at all, seeing as how I've run into you, Andy Dobson. Only yesterday I was talking to your teachers, and they told me that you're leading Lucy astray and that her performance at school is clearly suffering."

"Don't say that, Sergeant."

"Don't try to be get smart with me! I haven't been promoted to Sergeant yet."

"Ah, but you will, never fear. All you need is a little patience."

"Andy Dobson, one of these days I'm going to lose my patience and give you a good thrashing. And remember, I've been authorised by that saintly woman, your mum."

"Ah . . . I can just imagine. Mum is always first when it comes to a punch-up."

"Anyhow, you might as well know that I've asked your teachers not to let you sit at the same desk as Lucy until you come to your senses. Damned good-for-nothing little scoundrel!"

This delightful scene is repeated nearly every day. Lucy's father seems like a gruff man, but, he's a really good sort who is very fond of Andy and looks on him nearly as a son.

Harry Catlett was also a close friend of Andy's father, Steve, and, after his death, Harry had taken the boy's interests very much to heart. He has been on duty in Whitechapel for so long that he truly has become an institution, well known and respected by one and all. Nobody messes him around. The local toughs fear him and try to stay out of his way when they can. His fifteen stone of pure muscle don't encourage anyone to—so to speak—step on his toes.

In class, Andy tells Lucy the story of his meeting with the young Italian and their decision to go and have a look at room 4 on the first floor.

Lucy isn't all that enthusiastic, but she swears that she will never let him go anyplace without her. They will have to make up some excuse for her to spend the night at the Jack-in-the-Box so she can join them.

Quick as a flash, Andy comes up with a story; he is a past master in the art of lying. "You can say that we have to study late, and that then you're going to sleep at our place."

Lucy says she thinks it might be a good idea.

Right after this, they are shushed by the teacher and aren't allowed to talk until school is out.

X

At tea with Granddad Bob, Andy tries more than once to tackle the question of the mysterious room in the hope that he might learn something—every attempt fails. Mum had probably scolded the old boy again.

Today, the new lodger from room 5 comes down to tea too—a distinguished-looking man named Hugo Drabber.

Andy finds him to be looking really very nice in his tweed suit.

He says he has come down from Devonshire. His deportment is impeccable, his manners, those of a true gentleman. He tells them that he has been for many years in the service of a land owner and that he has always been in charge of running the estate. Now that he has retired, he has come to London to visit some relatives.

He really is a most likable person.

He confesses that he had a hobby: kites. As soon as his work allowed, he was off by himself across the fields, flying the kites that he himself had made. Running through the fields alone, he says, made him feel like a boy again.

"There's nothing like a brisk run in the country in the early morning ahead of a fine kite to make you forget your worries."

What an unusual character Mr. Hugo Drabber is.

Hugo Drabber, thinks Andy, *what a funny name!*

But then, everything about this rather tubby, retired country gentleman seems rather funny. Funny and old-fashioned, starting from his clothes: a loud, green-and-yellow-checked jacket with a rounded collar; a tailored waistcoat; a stiff collared shirt with a bow tie; and a pair of trousers made of the same material as the jacket. His heavy dark mustache, which he keeps stroking with his large, coarse hands, makes him look as if he belongs in another time: a face that seems to have sprung from one of those nineteenth-century paintings that are discovered in some attic every now and again.

Andy finds it hard to picture him racing across the landscape with a kite. Still, he has taken a liking to ol' Drabber.

When the meal is over, Granddad and Mr. Drabber both light up their pipes and start talking about the old days, the war, and about how much London has changed in the last few years.

Going into the kitchen to fetch some brandy for the diners, Andy notices that his mum is talking to someone. At once, he crouches behind the door to eavesdrop—one of his favourite pastimes.

From there, he can't see who she is speaking to but a moment later he recognises the voice of Lucy's father.

"Emma, I don't want to frighten you, but we have been notified of the presence in the city of a dangerous serial killer.

"He is a very strange character with a mania for the exploits of Jack the Ripper. We know hardly anything about him—haven't even got a description—but, according to my superiors, because of his obsession, he would very likely be attracted to this area and to this—"

"And *maybe* even to my guest house," Emma breaks in. "Come off it, Harry! It all sounds very

— 66 —

silly! Sometimes you men seem like a bunch of kids to me. Bob spends his days filling Andy's head with complete rubbish, always the same old stuff—monsters and butchers. And the result? I'll tell you straightaway! My son's performance at school is poor, not to say disastrous. While I'm trying to play down Andy's strange powers, his grandfather is playing them up. I do not want everyone to regard my son as some kind of freak or, worse still, as an idiot. And now you come along, warning me about an improbable comeback by Jack the Ripper. Don't you think it's a bit much? You, too—just like my poor Steve—you're a dreamer. Just like he was, you're obsessed with these old stories."

"You're not being fair, Emma," replies Harry. "You know very well that I look after your family like it's my own . . . and anyway, it's something I promised Steve. He would have done the same for my family if something had happened to me. He was my best friend."

"I'm sorry, Harry," says Emma, her tone softening. "I'm just a little edgy—too many things to look after here. I'm all alone."

"Emma, I know you're a very courageous woman, but, I beg you, if you see anything out of the ordinary, don't hesitate to call me at any hour of the day or night."

"You're always so good to us," says Emma, "and I swear if I see some sinister character in blood-soaked clothes, you'll be the first to know!"

Andy had heard enough, so he went into the kitchen with a casual "hi there," and, after taking down a bottle of brandy, headed back toward the dining room.

A serial killer! thinks Andy, as he hurries along the corridor separating him from the dining room, *another Jack!*

Andy is beside himself; he can think of nothing more exciting than what he has just heard. *A fine cure for boredom in this bloody hotel where nothing interesting ever happens*, he thinks.

He feels like a combination of private detective and medieval knight. Ah yes! because he, too, has a damsel to defend. Improbable, fantastic scenarios begin to crowd into his head—images made up of less-than-human eyes staring from the darkness, sharp-edged blades waiting to slake their insatiable thirst for blood, and, above all, defenceless damsels eager to thank their rescuers with a kiss. By an odd chance, every one of these imaginary damsels in distress has the angelic features of Lucy.

"Mr. Drabber got sleepy and he went to his room," says Granddad Bob, pouring himself a good stiff glass of brandy. "Nice chap, though."

Straightaway, Andy informs him of what he has heard Mr. Catlett telling his mum.

Old Bob is visibly upset and after scolding him for listening behind doors, decides that another large glass of brandy will help to ease the strain.

It should be said that, for Granddad, every event represents a chance to—in his words— "ease the strain" by downing a good stiff glass of brandy or gin, rather than a pint of beer.

As happens nearly every afternoon, Andy's bedroom is the scene of Lucy's futile attempts to get him to study. Some hopes! After what he has just heard, his entire attention is focused on how to get into room 4.

Poor Lucy. She is just as unsuccessful in trying to persuade him not to undertake the expedition, which she considers both crazy and dangerous.

"Andy Dobson! Your mum would skin you alive after roasting you over a slow fire if she knew what you are planning with that Italian friend of yours."

"She doesn't have to be told, my dear Lucy Catlett. Come to think of it, you've given me an idea. Let's go see Massimo."

When they enter Massimo's room, they find him buried deep in an enormous history book, busily making notes.

"Massimo, this is my friend Lucy."

"Ah, sit down, my friends. You've come at just the right moment. I was expecting you. Pleased to meet you, Lucy."

Pushing two large armchairs together, he invites them to sit down and, after offering them some orange juice in two plastic cups, he begins to speak.

In the faint light of a single lamp standing on the desk, the three of them have the air of conspirators intent on hatching God knows what devilish undertaking.

"Before moving on to the operational stage of our plan, I want to give you a short history lesson and I hope that your little girlfriend is not too squeamish."

"Don't worry," says Andy. "She's one of those plucky types—she doesn't even cry at the dentist."

"Dead right," says Lucy with ill-concealed pride, "I don't cry even with that horrid Dr. Broquette, and she always hurts me something terrible."

"It's really so, Massimo," Andy adds for good measure. "That tub of lard always hurts her awfully, and Lucy never complains. She's as gutsy as they come is my pal Lucy!"

"If you ask me, she's not a real dentist at all." remarks Lucy.

"Okay . . . okay," Massimo breaks in, "she probably bought her degree. I get the distinct feeling that you're not all that fond of her, but that's not what we're here to talk about."

Massimo lights a cigarette and perches himself on the edge of the still unmade bed and resumes speaking, while the two little friends gaze at him, curiosity mingled with impatience.

"Imagine yourselves in 1888. This area is a tangle of dirty alleys, populated by nearly a million people, poor folk who, as you know, try to survive by doing the strangest, the humblest of jobs.

"Not far from here is the London of the upper classes, the London of the exclusive Pall Mall clubs, of horse-drawn carriages. That sort of people don't come over here except for brief, nocturnal excursions in search of cheap thrills. Around here, the women sell themselves for a few pence. And it is just nearby, near the Whitechapel Road

Police Station, that our Jack strikes for the first time. On the night of August 31, 1888, at about four in the morning, a man by the name of Charles Cross, a carter, was on his way to work. As he was passing by Buck's Row, something grabbed his attention and he stopped. Tossed into an alleyway like some worthless piece of junk was the corpse of 'one of those,' Mary Ann Nichols—her throat had been slit and her abdomen cut open."

Hearing these things, an expression of horror and disgust spreads over the features of the children.

"I told you it was a pretty grim story!" says Massimo, realising from their expressions that he is making them quite upset. He continues: "A few days later another scene, not unlike the first, presents itself to the horrified eyes of a policeman on his night beat. In another alley, Hanbury Street, right next to the Police Station, the completely eviscerated cadaver of Annie Chapman, another prostitute, is found. The crime had been carried out with a savagery unprecedented in previous cases."

"How revolting!" says Lucy, turning pale. "But who was this Annie Chapman?"

"One of those unfortunates who populated the East End in those days—forty-five years old, with tuberculosis and a certain penchant for alcohol. She made her living as best she could: living by her wits . . ."

"Poor thing." murmurs Lucy in a barely audible voice. "Those must have been awful times."

"After these two cases," continues Massimo, "Scotland Yard began to investigate, mobilising more than eight thousand policemen who were sent through the entire East End with a fine-tooth comb, day and night, but to no avail. Until, on the night of September 30, 1888, friend Jack pulled off a double."

"A double?" the two youngsters exclaim in unison, only to remain wide-eyed and openmouthed an instant later.

"Yes. That night, Jack mutilated the bodies of two more women: Elizabeth Stride and Catherine Eddowes. The two corpses were found a short distance from each another, as the crow flies. The crimes were committed in the space of a few hours, but the method was different because something probably happened."

"Describe it properly," Andy demands. "The story's getting really interesting."

"Okay," continues Massimo. "Let's talk about Elizabeth Stride. She was a woman of Swedish origin, about forty-five, like Annie Chapman. She worked as a part-time prostitute, too, in order to pay for bed and board in some decrepit lodging house in the area. That night, at about one in the morning, a jewel merchant, a certain Louis Diemschutz, was just turning into Dutfield's Yards in his gig drawn by a little pony. All of a sudden the little animal stopped dead and refused to go on. So, after getting down off his gig in the dark— because in those days the streets weren't well lighted—this man realised that something on the ground was blocking the way. At first he thought it was some drunk who had fallen asleep in the middle of the road, a thing which, at that time, was by no means unusual. So he went to a nearby pub The Workingman's Club to ask for help.

"A short time later he came back with two customers, Isaac Kozebrodsky and Morris Eagle, and, lighting up the area with a lantern, they discovered that the thing blocking the carriage was the lifeless body of Elizabeth Stride.

"The corpse, which was still warm, showed a single, long slash across the throat from ear to ear but not the mutilations of the previous crimes. Why was that, do you think?" Massimo asks them.

"Because Jack was disturbed by something and didn't have time to carve her up!" yells Andy, almost like a contestant on a quiz show.

"Good man! And it was probably the arrival of the gig that disturbed him. In fact, Mr. Diemschutz later gave evidence that, in the few moments following the discovery of the body, the pony was very skittish, as if it perceived the presence of someone in that dark courtyard. Jack was probably still there."

"Wow! Isn't that exciting? Better than going to the movies," exclaims Andy, turning toward Lucy, looking for confirmation.

"Absolutely not. I think it's disgusting." she replies, putting a damper on his enthusiasm.

"At any rate," Massimo goes on, ignoring the children's remarks, "a few hours later, our mysterious assassin got his own back. In Mitre Square he made a butchery of the body of his fourth victim, Catherine Eddowes.

"At that point Scotland Yard is completely baffled. They go by guesswork, investigating places where people use sharp tools in their professions, given the skill with which Jack cut his victims into pieces. So they arrest scores of people, all of them immigrants: Poles, Russians, Armenians—all cobblers, barbers, tailors, butchers—in short, anyone who uses sharp instruments in their trade."

"And did they catch him?" gulps Lucy.

"No, no! They had to let them all go because they had nothing on them. Jack struck one last time before vanishing into thin air, but this time his method differed from his previous crimes. The scene was no longer an alleyway but inside a house. Mary Jane Kelly was a pretty girl of about twenty-five. Unlike the first four who were a bit long in the tooth, she had no need to walk the streets in order to find 'friends.' She had a little room on the first floor of a boardinghouse, at 22 Batty Street."

"But . . . we're at 22 and this is Batty Street!" shouts Lucy, springing to her feet as if someone has suddenly lit a bonfire under her.

It takes a few minutes to get Lucy to settle down; all she can say is that she wants to go home. In the end, Andy succeeds in comforting her.

Lucy sits down again and begins holding on tight to Andy's arm—and, as we know, this makes him very happy.

After this brief interruption, Massimo proceeds with his tale, and the pair of them continue to listen to him in stunned silence.

"Well then, the police who entered the room that, now it can be said, is room four, came face-to-face with a scene even more bloodcurdling than the others: the walls of the wretched little room are spattered from top to bottom with the poor woman's blood, almost as if the killer had amused himself by tracing sinister, meaningless signs on the walls—using a most unusual kind of ink.

"Hang on," he adds, opening one of the books lying on the desk. "If you like, I'll read you the report filed by Dr. Thomas Bond, the Scotland Yard coroner, who was called to the scene to make out a report on the crime."

"Interesting." observes Andy, affecting a certain coolness so as to impress Lucy.

"Well, I find it revolting. Actually, I'd be very grateful if you would spare me the details which I bet are enough to make me vomit."

Neither Andy nor Massimo pays any attention, so all Lucy can do is listen petrified to Massimo as he reads the coroner's report.

"The body was lying naked in the middle of the bed . . . the axis of the body inclined to the left. . . . The head was turned on the left cheek. The whole of the surface of the abdomen and thighs was removed and the abdominal cavity emptied of its viscera. . . . The arms mutilated by several jagged wounds, and the face hacked beyond recognition of the features. The viscera were found in various parts viz: the uterus and kidneys with one breast under the head, the other breast by the right foot, the liver between the feet, the intestines and the spleen by the left side of the body. . . .

"The bed clothing at the right corner was saturated with blood, and on the floor beneath was a pool of blood covering about two feet square. The wall by the right side of the bed and in a line with the body was marked by blood which had struck it in a number of separate splashes. . . . The blood was produced by the severance of the carotid artery, which was the cause of death.

"The face was gashed in all directions, the nose, cheeks, eyebrows and ears being partly removed. . . . The intercostals between the fourth, fifth, and sixth ribs were cut through and the contents of the thorax visible through the openings. . . . The pericardium was open below and the heart absent. In the abdominal cavity there was some partly digested food of fish and potatoes, and similar food was found in the remains of the stomach attached to the intestines. . . ."

"How cheerful!" Lucy suddenly explodes; evidently she's had quite enough.

"That's it for now, Massimo! You've made me sick," says Andy.

"But I'm not finished yet!" protests Massimo. "I still have to read the letters and the poems that

Jack started sending to the police and the news-papers—ridiculing both. Let me go on.

"This time the suspicions of the police fell on one of the lodgers, a strange man, a certain Dr. Francis Tumblety; but when they tried to contact him, he had already disappeared in haste, leaving all his bags and baggage behind in his room. That was the last crime, because Jack had van-ished without trace.

"As I told you, during the investigations Jack made fun of the police by writing ghoulish verses and letters and sending them to Scotland Yard. Listen, I found one here in this book."

Massimo gets up off the bed and, opening the old volume lying on the desk, reads a few lines to the two kids who, in the meantime, have been left gaping and speechless:

> *"I'm not a butcher, me*
> *Nor a sailor from the sea.*
> *Nor a nasty little Jew,*
> *But a friend who's close to you.*
> *Signed: Jack The Ripper."*

"Did you like that?" says Massimo.

"I don't like anyone who has anything against Jewish people," replies Andy thoughtfully.

"Do we really have to hear this?" chimes Lucy.

"Wait." says Massimo, "Just listen to this, then!"

"Eight little whores, with no hope of heaven,
Gladstone may save one, then there'll be
seven.
Seven little whores beggin' for a shilling,
One stays in Henage Court, then there's a
killing.
Six little whores, glad to be alive,
One sidles up to Jack, then there are five.
Four and whore rhyme aright,
So do three and me,
I'll set the town alight
Ere there are two.
Two little whores, shivering with fright,
Seek a cosy doorway in the middle of the
night.
Jack's knife flashes, then there's but one,
And the last one's the ripest for Jack's idea of
fun."

As soon as he finishes reading these lines, Massimo is also visibly upset and heaves a deep sigh. After replacing the dusty tome on the desk, he sits down on the bed once more.

A deathly pallor had spread over the faces of the two children.

Lucy's fingernails are sunk deep into Andy's arm and she is clinging to him for all she is worth, like someone dangling from a branch over the edge of a cliff. The three of them remain in silence for long, interminable minutes; none of them has the courage or the desire to remark on what they have just heard.

Once more it is Lucy who, having recovered her wits, breaks the silence. "This story is absolutely . . . absolutely revolting, so there!"

"On the contrary, I find it fascinating," says Andy with a trace of recklessness in his voice.

"Andy," Massimo ventures, "I was thinking that those wonderful and strange powers of yours might come in very handy—if you agree, of course—in trying to understand more about this horrible story. Look, I've been doing research in the university library and I've read that there are people like you who can not only feel sensations by handling objects belonging to others, but can even *see* people and places in their minds. Of course, this happens with older people in whom these powers are particularly well developed. From what you told me—and because of your age—you may need some help to make your powers extend that far. I don't know. Anyhow, I read that there are certain compounds that amplify perceptions—you know, compounds that are kind of hallucinogenic. I was reading about experiments where the subjects being analysed talked about authentic journeys through the memories of other people. It would be great to be able to do this, but you'd have to agree to it," Massimo concludes a little hesitantly.

"Andy Dobson!" screams Lucy. "You're not going to do something like that!"

"Go on with what you were saying, Massimo," Andy says, paying no attention to Lucy. "I find this very interesting."

"You see, Andy," Massimo continues, "I could get some of this compound from a French doctor friend of mine who works in a hospital and, if you agree—"

Andy doesn't even let him go on. "Okay, you get the medicine and we'll do the experiment, but first we've got to get hold of something from that period, an object that belonged to someone who had something to do with the crime."

"That's where I come in!" replies Massimo triumphantly, taking a gleaming steel picklock out of a drawer.

"This gadget will get us into the room that used to belong to poor Mary Jane Kelly, and if it's true that no one has set foot in there for more than a hundred years, we have a real chance of finding something that will help us. You agree, too, don't you, Lucy?"

"All I can say is that the two of you must have a couple of screws loose. I don't care what *you* get up to, Massimo, but as for you, Andy Dobson, if you intend to go on with this madness and take drugs without knowing where they come from, then let me tell you, I'll never, *ever* speak to you again."

When Lucy is really cross she calls Andy by his full name and this time she really *is* mad.

Long discussions between the two of them are necessary before Lucy's resistance is overcome—

and Andy, who knows her very well, finally succeeds.

"All right, then, I'll go along with you on this insane adventure but on one condition: I've got the same rights as you two. I go wherever you go."

"It's a deal! Now we can go," exults Andy, and he begins slapping Massimo on the back. Massimo himself is a little less enthusiastic about the whole thing.

"First, take this and have a look at it," says Massimo, handing him the old volume from which he had just read out the Ripper's two macabre bits of verse. "Seeing as the thing seems to interest you very much, here you'll find the letters Jack wrote to the press and the police. They're really quite interesting."

"Ah! Most intriguing," Lucy observes ironically, "the sort of stuff that keeps you awake nights, I imagine."

In the end, they decide that the visit to room 4 should take place that very night. Massimo carefully arranges on the desk the objects that they will be taking with them: the picklock, two electric torches, a small camera, and a large blue canvas bag.

They part after agreeing that Massimo will come to Andy's room after midnight.

There is no more talk of studying. Andy is far too excited about what is going to take place later that night.

XII

When Lucy enters Andy's room carrying a plate with two enormous slices of marmalade cake on it, he doesn't even notice; he is engrossed in a computer game.

"Snack time!" she proclaims, to attract his attention.

He doesn't turn a hair.

"What game is that? A new one?"

"Hmm? Oh, yeah!" Andy replies absently as if he has suddenly become aware of her presence. "It's fantastic. It's called Carmageddon. You're the driver of the car and you've got to run down the passersby, the more you plaster against the wall, the more points you score."

Lucy glares at the computer screen with her usual expression of disapproval. She is staring at a hurtling vehicle and watching the poor pedestrians who, from time to time, after bouncing off the bonnet of the car, are crushed under the wheels with spine-chilling screams. At every scream from one of the poor pedestrians, a crimson stain appears on the screen with a sinister *splat*! that makes Lucy flinch every time. She detests this kind of computer game.

It takes fifty-two pedestrians crushed like flies, and Lucy's threat that she would go home, to convince Andy to switch off the computer.

The two of them sit down on the bed and make short work of the two slices of marmalade cake.

"I told your mum that we would be studying late, so she rang my house to say I'd be sleeping here."

"Okay!" says Andy, swallowing his last mouthful of cake. "I can't wait for midnight to come to get into that room."

"But aren't you a bit scared?"

"Are you?"

"A bit, yes," says Lucy.

"In that case, I'm a bit scared, too."

Andy decides not to tell Lucy of the conversation he had overheard that afternoon about the serial killer. *Poor thing*, he thinks, *she'd be even more freaked out.*

Then they start imagining what they are likely to find behind that door.

"We might find gold and jewels, the loot from God knows what crime or maybe important, compromising secret documents!"

"In which case," says Lucy, "the gold and jewels are mine and I'll leave the compromising documents to you. But something tells me that all we'll find is cobwebs and beetles. And if things go wrong, maybe a right telling off by our folks if they find out!"

Having eaten their fill, they lie side by side on their backs holding hands, lost in reverie. The streetlamps come on at dusk and the sunset surprises Andy. He gets up.

A little groggy—she must have fallen asleep for a while—Lucy explores the space around her with her hand and meets no resistance.

When she half opens her eyes and realises that she is all alone in the room, she begins to feel uneasy. She hurriedly slips on her shoes, wondering where on earth Andy could have gone.

Idiot! she thinks, rubbing her eyes, *he knows perfectly well that I can't stand being left alone, especially in this creepy place, and yet he does it on purpose. As soon as you turn your back, he's gone.*

As she is reflecting on this, her eyes are searching the room, looking for some hint of what is going on, and her attention is caught by a large red stain on the floor right in the centre of the room.

She immediately feels her heart leap into her mouth, beating madly, and her breath comes in broken gasps.

With increasing dismay, she notices that the stain, which has all the characteristics of blood, is not the only one. Smaller ones, in orderly single file accompany it, giving the room an extremely sinister look.

In the muffled silence that encloses the scene Lucy is able to hear herself breathing or, rather, panting.

Her gaze, following the little spots, ends up at the bathroom door.

With short steps, holding her breath so as not to disturb the nameless demons that inhabit the house, she approaches the half-open door from which a weak light filters out. She has barely put her nose inside the bathroom, when *pow*! an enormous, slimy, wart-covered hand is suddenly thrust in her face. Lucy leaps backwards, loses her balance, and falls sprawling on the floor.

For several interminable seconds, with her eyes screwed shut so as not to see, she hopes it is just a dream. She decides to open her eyes slowly, hoping that she has made a mistake. But no! The huge arm is still there resting against the bathroom door which, only slightly ajar, allows nothing more to be seen.

Suddenly the long, repellent, skinny fingers that look like prehistoric talons start twitching nervously and drumming on the wood of the door. Lucy wants to scream, to run away, but instead she is unable to utter a sound or move a muscle.

The bathroom door suddenly springs open, and all that is left for the poor girl to do is to contemplate the triumphant face of Andy as he explodes in a loud belly laugh.

"This pure latex gauntlet is supposed to be the revolting hand of the *Monster from the Deserted Mine*! The book's quite good—the film . . . not so good."

Having said this, Andy strips off the rubber glove from his hand and tosses it across poor Lucy's legs. She is gaping at him in astonishment.

She doesn't say a word. She gets up off the floor. She goes up to Andy and after rewarding him with a sarcastic smile, turns her back on him for an instant, only to whip round again and hit him a clout that—*splat!*—plants itself like a suction cup on the unfortunate lad's face, wiping away his infuriating grin.

"Andy Dobson! You're hateful! You and your usual stupid tricks. . . . Is it possible that that's all you're good for?"

Five red fingers are neatly printed on Andy's cheek. He is still trying to figure out, with some difficulty, whether it was Lucy's gentle hand that had hit him or if the driver of the London-Glasgow Express had lost control and the train had left the rails and crashed into his freckled face!

"Lucy, that hurt!"

"And that's nothing. . . . You deserve much worse after the fright you gave me."

Andy, realising that perhaps he has really overdone it, tries to play things down.

"Phew! You certainly pack a punch for such a small girl."

"It's the fear that does it. I suppose you'll be happy to hear that I nearly wet myself!"

"Aw, come on! It's only a little rubber hand. . . ."

"It's totally revolting!" replies Lucy, putting the gauntlet on her hand. "What about all that blood on the floor?"

"Oh! That's ketchup!" says Andy. "I nearly used the whole lot."

As he cleans the room of the tomato stains, using a scrubbing brush under the Lucy's watchful eye, Andy has all the time he needs to reflect on the wisdom of playing practical jokes.

XIII

Emma's culinary touch has not been particularly felicitous today in the kitchen. It's always the same whenever something is worrying her.

The slices of roast beef neatly arranged on the metal tray in the centre of the table do not look particularly inviting. Lucy barely tastes hers, and Andy, who is too excited at the prospect of an event-filled evening after supper, eats only some mashed potato.

Granddad Bob and Mr. Drabber hold other views and do battle over the roast beef to the very last slice. Emma never seems to eat.

"My compliments, Mrs. Dobson!" says Hugo Drabber, speaking with his mouth full. "This is the finest roast beef I have tasted in a long time."

"But he isn't 'tasting' it," whispers Andy in Lucy's ear. "He's polishing it off."

Lucy can hardly keep from laughing out loud when Granddad very gravely informs all present,

"My bottle of ketchup has mysteriously vanished. Where are we going to end up at this rate! You can't even leave a bottle of tomato sauce unguarded without having it disappear. There's always queer things happening in this house. . . . Your mother doesn't want to admit it, but this place has a curse on it."

Having assured Granddad of his innocence, Andy hazards a guess that the culprit might be the ghost of some ancestor. "Maybe it's old Alistair himself having some fun playing tricks on you. After all, didn't they use to call him 'the Joker'?"

No one answers him.

After duly honouring the chocolate cake that Emma always makes when Lucy is invited, the two youngsters say good night to the company and withdraw.

In Andy's room, they try various ways of whiling away the time. They are both very nervous, even though they don't show it. With hardly a word to each other, they listen to some music, watch a bit of television, and leaf through some magazines.

Lucy finally breaks the silence. "If your mum knew what you're planning to do . . . I don't dare to think about it; *and* I don't dare think about something else, either."

"What?" asks Andy, as he puts on his sneakers. "That she will tell my dad straightaway and then, *good-bye* pocket money, and *good-bye* summer holidays."

"Everything will turn out fine, you'll see," says Andy, taking her by the hand.

She gazes at him with her big blue eyes and immediately afterwards presses her forehead against his for a brief instant.

"Forgive me for today. I hurt you, didn't I?"

"No, no. It's you who should forgive me! I must have given you a right scare."

"Let's not think about it anymore."

Andy had never told anyone, not even her, that he has already dreamed that, when they grow up, he is going to marry this girl with the rosy cheeks who is always so lovely and so sweet.

Lucy has never told anyone, not even him, but she has secretly decided that, when she grows up, she is going to marry this impudent yet sweet prankster with the freckled face.

Neither of them has ever told the other, yet both of them already know. And so they wait for

Massimo to come, watching TV and holding hands.

Shortly before midnight, Massimo knocks softly on Andy's door. An odd sort, this Massimo—he seems to be dressed more for a commando operation in enemy territory than for a visit to a hotel room!

His face is smooth and freshly shaven and he's wearing a black, close-fitting polo-neck sweater and a woollen watch cap. He looks like a character out of an action movie—totally different from how he appeared to Andy at first, a rather awkward-looking young student with an unshaven face.

"Aha! so it's true love, then. I didn't know you were engaged!" Massimo teases. Lucy's glare, which by itself is worth a thousand words, goes right through him.

Massimo gets the message straightaway and, after lighting a cigarette, he opens the large bag that he has brought with him. After switching on and off the two torches to test them, he says, "Right, then, let's go over the situation. We're going to go down the corridor, being very careful to make no noise, and then, taking the stairs we go up to the first floor."

"I know how to get there," replies Andy in a sarcastic tone. "I've lived here all my life."

"Okay!" says Lucy with her customary determination. "Let's go and have it done with."

The three leave the room without saying a word and take great care not to make a sound. At night, the corridors of the Jack-in-the-Box, dimly lit to save electricity, seem very sinister. Lucy has the feeling that the eyes of the stuffed animals that crowd the walls are following her, but she is careful not to show her feelings to the other two.

In complete silence, they move along the corridor and find themselves facing the stairs leading to the first floor. Andy casts a glance toward the kitchen a few paces away—near where his mum's room is. A thin pencil beam of light filters from under her door.

"Mum's still awake," Andy observes. "she's probably going over the day's accounts. As usual, she'll be upset because the takings are so low."

After a brief pause, they start up the stairs, and the worn wooden treads started creaking and groaning as if, tired after years of hard work, they have decided to give way beneath the weight of the amateur sleuths.

A couple of steps from the top, they suddenly stop when they hear confused, off-key singing coming from the end of the first floor corridor.

"Hold it!" whispers Massimo, who is leading the group.

Going forward alone, he climbs the final few steps that separate them from the corridor and peeps round the corner in the direction from which the singing is heard. After a few seconds he turns to Andy and Lucy and gestures for them to take a look for themselves. Though the light is very dim, all three recognise Mr. Hugo Drabber, who is walking toward his room, the one next to room 4.

From the exaggerated way he is waving his arms and from his unsteady walk, it is clear that he has been visiting Granddad Bob, who must certainly have offered him a goodly portion of his reserve of choice liquors.

"Your grandfather has found himself a friend," Lucy whispers, "they must have the same hobby—gin and beer."

"You're forgetting the brandy," Andy whispers gleefully.

The three stand watching him as he makes his way along the corridor, weaving from one wall to the other in search of support. When he gets to the door of his room, he leans his head against it, momentarily interrupting his mumbled song. Then he starts rummaging around in his pocket and begins to hum again. After several futile attempts at inserting the key in the lock, he finally manages it and enters his room, slamming the door behind him.

For an instant the light from his room illuminates the corridor, and the three draw back quickly for fear of being seen.

"Not to worry," Andy says, "he's so full of gin he wouldn't see an elephant if it appeared in front of him. So, do we go on or are we supposed to spend the night in this corridor?"

"Right!" Lucy breaks in, rather peeved. "We've got to go to school in the morning."

"Lucy, do you feel up to staying here alone while we open the door?" Massimo asks.

"All right," she says. "Anyway, I will be able to see both of you from here, won't I?"

Massimo and Andy set off slowly along the corridor and, as they go, Andy waves good-bye to Lucy. The two, after a careful look round, bend down in front of the door to room 4.

"They never even let me get close to this door." says Andy, stroking the wood. Even the door to room 4 looks different from the others. The Dobsons had evidently preferred to ignore the very existence of the room—the proof being that no one had even bothered to polish the door. Unlike the other doors, this one is dull and covered with little holes that betray the presence of woodworm.

From time to time, Andy turns his gaze toward Lucy, whom he can make out puffing with irritation and worry in the gloom. With Andy directing the light of one of the torches at the lock of the door, Massimo begins to fiddle with the picklock.

"Look here a sec!"

Andy, who is always in the mood for a joke, has pointed the beam of light under his chin and, after inflating his cheeks like a frog and making his eyes bulge out, assumed a ghostly look and tries to attract Massimo's attention.

"If you don't shine the light on the lock, I'll won't be able to figure this out. After all, not being a professional burglar, it's not as if I know much about locks."

After Massimo's gentle reprimand, Andy starts wondering again about what they might find in a room where nobody has set foot for more than a hundred years. He begins to have wild fantasies about what might lie hidden on the other side of the door. He is distracted by the broad grin that lights up Massimo's face when he manages to spring the ancient lock.

"*Voilà*! The thing is done, *monsieur*!" he says with barely concealed pride.

"You going in first, Massimo?"

"Yes . . . no. It doesn't matter."

"Uh . . . you go first, then." Andy decides.

In the meantime, at Andy's signal, Lucy has hurried down the corridor to join them.

"Ready, then?" whispers Massimo, leaning a hand against the door.

They spend long moment staring in absorbed silence at the door until Massimo, after switching on the second torch, slowly turns the handle. . . .

The door opens wide, creaking just like in a horror film.

The first sensation they are aware of is the strong smell: one of those smells that you can't put a name to—a mixture of something sickly sweet; of old, damp furniture; and windows that haven't been opened in years. In spite of the fact that no one had set foot inside for a long time, the room, from what they can see in the light from the torches, does not look all that bad. Broad planks of white wood nailed across the windows prevent them from being opened; on the right, some furniture and a few chairs are piled up. Dust and cobwebs reign supreme.

"Revolting!" Lucy says in a low voice. "It's filthy and probably full of rats, too."

Aiming his torch to the left, Andy sees another piece of furniture: a large wardrobe made of dark wood. On either side of it are untidy mounds of assorted household odds and ends: wicker baskets, piles of old newspapers, and other useless junk.

Sitting on top of one of these piles of paper lies an old leather bag completely covered in dust—a

Gladstone bag like those country doctors used to carry years ago when making house calls.

"Look, Massimo," Andy whispers, pouncing on the old bag. "It's got initials on it."

Right away Massimo, too, shines his torch in that direction. Andy is pointing at two small gilt letters, half hidden by the dust, which embellish the bag. "F. T. Hmm . . . interesting."

Without another word, Massimo takes the bag from the boy's hands and stuffs it into the big blue canvas sack.

"F. T. stands for Francis Tumblety, doesn't it?" Andy presses him excitedly.

"Anything's possible. . . . We'll have a look later on." The Italian cuts him short.

All of a sudden, Lucy lets out a cry that she immediately stifles. "I saw something! Yuck—a rat."

Andy shines his torch into the corner where Lucy is pointing, and immediately dozens of enormous rats, their eyes gleaming, start leaping all over the room.

Massimo holds off the ones that get too close—or at least tries to do so—by lashing out with savage kicks that miss most of the time. Lucy clutches Andy's arm and begins to whimper quietly so that Andy is forced to put his hand over her mouth to keep her from waking anyone. Lucy is a brave girl, but if there is one thing she absolutely can't stand it is those horrible animals—rats. Her mum always said that they carry all sorts of diseases.

For this reason she even detested being in the countryside. Years before, in a mill, she had encountered a mouse. It was one of those tiny mice with an attractive little snout that lives among the sacks of flour. To no avail her mum and dad tried to explain—to get her to understand—that it was harmless. She cried her heart out for hours and refused to listen.

But these are truly abominable beasts. And how mad they are! Some of the more aggressive ones try to attack the two kids but are driven back with the aid of a battered lady's handbag that Andy has hastily snatched up off the floor and is now brandishing like a club. But the rats— heedless of the blows they receive, fearless, and as if more maddened—continue to attack, squeaking and squealing like things possessed.

"These rats are huge! They're the size of cats! We've got to get out of here!" Andy implores, as the foul beasts continue to race madly about making a tremendous racket.

A few moments later and without a word—as if they have read each one another's minds—the three of them find themselves back in the corridor. Massimo, closing the door behind him, heaves a long sigh of relief.

"We're right duffers!" says Massimo. "Here we are on the trail of a bloodthirsty killer and we let ourselves be scared by a few rats."

"A *few* rats?" Andy repeats with resentment. "Those aren't rats, they're wild beasts—vampires. Just think!"

"Well anyway, we got something for our trouble," says Massimo, taking off his cap and drying the sweat that has beaded on his forehead.

He takes the handbag from Andy and shoves it into the canvas sack along with the Gladstone they found. Very cautiously they descend the stairs and return to Andy's room. Lucy is as white as a sheet and is perspiring so much that she looks as if she had fallen into a swimming pool. She doesn't say a word. As soon as she enters the room she throws herself down on the bed. "I'm absolutely worn out. I feel like someone who's just run a marathon."

Massimo dumps the contents of the sack onto the table. The three stare in silence at the handbag and the Gladstone for some seconds, until Andy decides that the time has come to take a look at what is inside them.

Massimo's hands are trembling with excitement as he snaps open the lock and the contents of the Gladstone tumble out on the table. "But, they're doctor's instruments!" he says, surprised.

"So. I was right!" Andy shouts. "It's got the initials F. T. It's full of medical instruments—it's got to be Francis Tumblety's bag."

"Could be." Massimo replies, still rummaging around in the bag to make sure there is nothing left inside. Lined up on the table are some scalpels, various empty glass vials stopped up with cotton, a stethoscope, and a copy of an old newspaper—the *Daily News*, to be exact.

"What is the date of that paper?" Andy asks.

Massimo unfolds the pages of the old newspaper in search of a date. "Gosh! November 1888."

"Now have a look in the handbag!" Lucy exclaims.

Following Lucy's orders, Andy finds himself holding two small tortoiseshell combs and a few hairpins.

At once he shoots a glance of disappointment at Massimo, who, as if reading his thoughts, replies, "Well? What the devil were you expecting to find—the bedroom walls spattered with blood and a sheet of paper with Jack's confession duly witnessed by a solicitor?"

"Of course not!" retorts Andy, a bit irritated. "And yet, the Gladstone is important—that Tumblety fellow . . . what more do you know about him, exactly?"

Massimo replies promptly enough: "Tumblety's life is filled with obscure areas—like all the rest of this grisly affair, come to think of it . . . There's a whole lot of mystery surrounding him, and the information we do have is contradictory. For example, up until a short time ago he was thought to have been born in Canada; but recently some of those who have studied his case have put forward the hypothesis that he was born in Ireland."

"Interesting." remarks Lucy.

Andy, on the contrary, says not a word; he is totally absorbed in Massimo's story.

"At any rate, one thing is for sure; without a shadow of doubt we are dealing with an out-and-out paranoid, quite independently of whether he was Jack-the-Ripper or not.

"From a very early age he was considered to be a clumsy, ill-mannered good-for-nothing slob and—"

"Hey! He's just like you, Andy!" Lucy says, as she begins to laugh.

Under the amused gaze of Massimo, who is enjoying the scene, Andy at first confines himself to directing a murderous glare at her—one of those intense looks that is designed to kill. Then, as if he had fully reflected on what he had just heard, he springs furiously to his feet.

"Shut up! I'm certainly not all that!"

But Lucy, not at all intimidated by his reaction, adds fuel to the fire "*You* shut up, *bone*head! Last year when we went on our trip to Brighton, you didn't change your shirt for three days—"

"Not true, snake in the grass!"

"No I'm not! It's true . . . I'll say it again, *bone*head!"

Andy and Lucy start to exchange insults with no holds barred and would probably have gone on this way for some time if Massimo, growing impatient, hadn't brought his fist down hard on the table reestablishing order. "Now then, if you want me to go on with the story, you just sit down and be quiet, otherwise I'll kick both your butts, okay?"

After a couple of seconds of complete silence, Massimo picks up the story of the mysterious Francis Tumblety. "As I was saying, our Francis was the son of James and Margaret Tumblety and the youngest of eleven children. From early adolescence he displayed a great interest in medicine. It was then that he started working as an apprentice in a little chemist's shop. Around about 1850, he moved to Detroit where he made his living as a herbalist and accumulated a tidy sum of money. He was first arrested in Montreal in 1857, but he wriggled out of that through a series of legal loopholes. He must have been of the roving kind because his presence was recorded in a whole series of places:

St. John, Montreal, Boston, San Francisco, New York, Pittsburgh, and lots of other cities.

"When the American Civil War broke out in 1861, he moved to Washington, D.C., where he passed himself off as a Union army surgeon. Apparently, he was not only extremely paranoid but also a hell of a yarn spinner. It seems that on occasion he claimed to be a close friend of President Abraham Lincoln and General Ulysses S. Grant. This mania for lies and invented friends in high places was to get him into serious trouble on more than one occasion. Later on, he was also arrested in connection with the investigation of President Lincoln's assassination, but his name was cleared. In Missouri he was arrested twice for wearing army uniforms and decorations that he wasn't entitled to. . . ."

"A perfect moron, in other words." Lucy laughs, sitting straight up on the bed.

"Much worse," replies Massimo, "A most dangerous and disturbed character."

"So how did he wind up in London?" Andy inquires.

"I'm coming to that," the Italian continues. "His decision to leave for Europe probably had something to do with his problems with the law. He went to London, Berlin, and Liverpool. In short, he travelled around a good deal and then he went to New York. In 1888 he returned to Liverpool, where he was arrested again.

"It was in 1888 that we also find our friend Francis in London—and here's the point that interests us most. Mary Jane Kelly was murdered on the night between November 8 and November 9, 1888. Three days later, on November 12, Tumblety was arrested under suspicion of being the author of the crime. A trial was set for December 10, but the bogus doctor was freed on bail on November 16.

"He never stood trial because, a few days after his release, on November 24, he escaped to France and, under the assumed name of Frank Townsend, he boarded the *La Bretagne*, bound for New York."

"Amazing," murmurs Andy, who is completely carried away by the tale.

"Pardon me," Lucy says, pointing a finger at Massimo, "I'm missing something here. Couldn't they simply have parcelled up this crazy in America and shipped him back to England?"

"Good point, Lucy. In point of fact, the American police put all ports under surveillance awaiting his arrival, and Scotland Yard sent a special agent to the States to track him down. When Inspector Byrnes of the New York police discovered that Francis Tumblety was in town and living in the house of a certain Mrs. McNamara, he had him followed and kept under observation. However, he couldn't arrest him as there was no proof of his guilt in connection with the London murders, and so he could not be extradited. On December 5, evading the surveillance of the New York police, Tumblety vanished into thin air.

"As the years passed every trace of him was lost and so was all interest in him. It was only after some years that Tumblety resurfaced in Rochester, New York, where he was living with his sister."

"And then? How did he end up?" Andy demands impatiently.

"Francis Tumblety died in St. Louis in 1903, and he took his secrets with him to the grave. There, that's the whole story."

"It's a really breathtaking story," says Lucy, jumping off the bed. "But if I don't get to sleep right away I'll end up in my grave. I'm dead tired."

"Women! Puh!" Andy jeers. "If it were a question of talking about clothes or gossip, they would stay up all night. But if the subject is serious, they get bored. It's really discouraging," he concludes, throwing up his arms in resignation.

"There's no point in being discouraged. Lucy's right. It's late now," says Massimo, glancing at his watch. "But tomorrow, with this stuff here, we can try our experiment, if, that is, your super-powers don't leave you in the lurch."

The clock shows it to be two in the morning and they decide it is time to get some rest. Massimo collects all his stuff. He says good night to his two young friends and sets off toward his room.

They are both exhausted, worn out by too much excitement for one evening. In a couple of minutes, Lucy is in and out of the bathroom wearing pretty, pink terrycloth pyjamas. She slips into Andy's bed while he, ever the gentleman,

curls up on the little sofa in the corner with a pil-
low and a blanket.

"Aren't you going to put on your pyjamas?"

"No, Lucy, I'm too tired," he replies with a
heavy sigh. "Anyhow, what's the point of getting
undressed when I'll have to put my clothes on
again in a few hours?"

"Ah! You really are an oddball—not even
going to take off your shoes?"

"The same goes for the shoes as for the
clothes." he replies, becoming more impatient.

"But you didn't even brush your teeth!" she
says, stubbornly attacking him. "Then you get all
sore if I tell you you're like Tumblety and—"

"*Lucy*! Andy bursts out, losing his temper like
a comedian. "If you don't go to sleep right away,
I'll really pretend I'm Tumblety . . . I'll get up and
chop you up into little bits just so I can get a few
hours sleep."

"Okay, Andy. G'night and a little kiss . . ."

"Good night!" Andy cuts short the conversation.

"And the little kiss?" Lucy murmurs softly.

"A kiss for you too, Lucy," Andy replies, by
now worn out by the discussion.

"Thanks Andy, and . . . good night."

But it was far from being a good night for the pair of them. It's a well-known fact that too much excitement disturbs a person's repose.

XIV

The next morning, Andy and Lucy find it hard to wake up; and throughout the morning they pretend to follow their lessons and avoid talking, even between themselves, about what had happened the previous night.

When school is over, the two part to go their separate ways; Lucy advises Andy to be very, very careful and, most especially, she begs him not to get involved in any strange experiments.

At three in the afternoon on the dot, Andy enters Massimo's room. The young man must have already been very busy, because the objects they had found the previous evening were neatly arranged on the table, all shiny and clean.

"Gotten over your fright?"

"Sure thing!" replies Andy, making himself comfortable.

Massimo starts talking about all sorts of things; and each time Andy asks him a specific question, he gives an evasive reply. He talks about the weather and about his studies, pacing nervously about the room, first tidying up some books then some knickknacks. Andy watches him with growing puzzlement until, after some hesitation, he decides to tackle the young man straight out.

"Masssimo, this is the third time you've tidied the books on that shelf and then shifted them again. Is there something wrong? You're acting like a nutter."

"I don't know, really, but this morning . . . You remember that compound I was telling you about, the one that would expand your powers? Well, this morning my French friend, who is a doctor at St. John's Hospital, gave me some of it."

"And so?" Andy interrupts. "We've already talked about it, haven't we? Let me take the pills and have done with it."

"Yes . . .well . . . ahem . . ." Massimo stammers. "You see, they're not actually pills—it's an injection. I didn't know . . . so you can refuse if you like."

Andy looks at him, his face pale. He loathes injections as much as Lucy loathes rats—a fear that has certainly been a source of embarrassment to him in the past.

Massimo stops talking. He nibbles at his nails. He can feel the pressure of Andy's gaze, which is becoming less reassuring by the minute. But once again Andy's curiosity proves stronger than his fear. All of a sudden, as if someone had set fire to a brazier under his bottom, he springs to his feet.

"What's the big deal? It's just a tiny injection. I mean, nobody's going to get killed!" he exclaims but without much conviction.

He hasn't yet finished his sentence when he sees Massimo take a little vial containing a blue, fluorescent fluid, then a tiny, disposable plastic syringe from a small leather case.

"Where did you learn to give injections?" Andy inquires, in an attempt to reassure himself.

"I learned while I was doing my national service," Massimo replies.

Somewhat uneasily, Andy slowly rolls up the sleeve of his shirt and shuts his eyes so as not to see the needle as it sinks in under his skin. A few seconds later, the dense, blue fluid had already begun coursing through his veins.

After replacing the vial and the syringe in the case, Massimo takes a chair and settles himself alongside the armchair where Andy is sitting with his face as white as a sheet.

"The French doctor explained that the solution I've just injected contains an alkaloid with a mild hallucinogenic effect which, combined with what you will feel when you touch the objects I'm going to give you, should let you perceive more clearly and even visualise certain situations. It should take effect in a few seconds and last for about twenty minutes or so."

Having said this, he takes a length of cord and quickly ties Andy at the elbow to the arms of the heavy armchair. "Don't worry. This is just a precaution. You might have hallucinations—"

Taken off guard, Andy tries to protest, but he feels as if his tongue has been transformed into a slab of meat that completely fills his mouth. He tries to say something, but all that comes out is a couple of incomprehensible splutters. When Massimo is done tying his arms, Massimo takes the Gladstone bag, places it on Andy's lap, and wraps the boy's hands, which are still free, around it.

What a strange feeling! Radiating from the bag Andy can feel a sort of warmth which, increasing as it goes, rises up his arm, then along his neck toward his head. His throat is dry and squeezed shut as if gripped in a vise. Andy feels as if he is perched on top of a ballistic missile being launched at high speed, armchair and all.

Pressed against the back of the armchair, he is already unable to distinguish the outlines of his surroundings. When it seems to him that the unbearable acceleration is becoming less intense, he tries to open his eyes but finds that he can't!

Then follows a few interminable seconds of complete weightlessness . . . then he is plummeting so fast that he has a sensation of a hole in his stomach, just like the time he had reluctantly climbed aboard a roller coaster at a theme park— only this time he is travelling a thousand times faster.

All the while, a rather worried Massimo observes him sitting quite still, lashed to the armchair, with a petrified expression and eyes shut as if asleep.

Now Andy is falling, falling. . . . Down, down so quickly that he can't even tell for how long. . . .

XV

He opens his eyes only when it seems to him that the long descent has ended; but rather than his eyesight, it is his sense of smell that he notices first. A disgusting odour of stagnant water and rotting vegetables wafts up his nose like swamp gas.

He retches a couple of times when he sees where he is: curled up right in the middle of a pile of garbage comprised of rotting vegetables of every description. Only inches from his face, he can see enormous rats fighting over leftover scraps of something that looks far from inviting.

Raising his gaze, he sees a host of people, all looking very sad and very busy, bustling every which way like ants on an anthill. He stands up and, with total indifference to the passersby who seem to ignore him, he makes his way from the alley in the direction of what has every sign of being a main street.

There the crowd has multiplied—a sea of humanity made up of hungry, sickly looking people dressed in rags. He sees wooden stalls loaded with goods, and carts of poultry and coal, and huge barrels that zigzag through the throng.

He had no sooner stuck his nose out of the alley than a closed carriage drawn by four handsome horses very nearly crushes him up against the wall.

The coachman, in elegant livery atop his box, sweeps on, cursing and cracking his long whip in the air.

Just like in my dream, he thinks in total amazement. *But where am I?* Andy has the feeling that the crowds of people passing by him, coachman included, cannot see him at all.

That's funny, he thinks. *My body is solid . . . but it's invisible to all these people.*

He tries to get his head around his new status of invisibility, which, to tell the truth, bothers him quite a bit. Just to make sure, he starts jumping up and down awkwardly and grimacing grotesquely only inches away from the face of a decrepit cigar seller on the street corner.

Nothing doing, he thinks.

Even though he is hopping about like a lunatic, the old cigar lady seems to be more concerned with the cold than with his presence of which, in any case, she remains quite unaware. She just can't see him.

So Andy starts to wander aimlessly about the alleys. He sees things he has never seen before: horse-drawn carts transporting all sorts of goods—huge blocks of ice, foul-smelling fish, and fruits and vegetables. He sees some women on street corners winking at passersby, who often swear at them in reply. Other women are camped out in the doorways of their dingy dwellings, intent on nursing their babies. But one can see from their swollen bellies that they will soon produce yet more children, who are probably destined to live in even greater poverty.

Swarms of ragged, filthy kids are battling one another savagely for possession of some worthless object they have found in the trash. After a thorough roll in the mud, they fall exhausted and breathing hard, ignoring the scolding of their mothers, who soon tire of calling after them and leave them to their own devices.

The small girls, less aggressive, are busy skipping rope, confining themselves to insulting one another when the rope isn't swung properly or when one of them doesn't jump high enough.

There are very few men around in the streets; most of them are huddled in the dimly lit pubs—of which there are plenty in the area—drinking beer and playing whist.

One thing is sure, thinks Andy, *these people don't seem to be doing all that well. Quite the opposite. They all look pretty miserable.*

When an organ-grinder, with eyes as cold and blue as an iceberg, curses in Czech and frees his shoulders from the straps which serve to haul his instrument about, the whole street comes to life. As soon as he starts to turn the handle, a kind of music, as rickety as everything else in the neighbourhood, attracts the attention of the youngsters.

Andy stands there awhile enjoying the sights, which are really new to him—boys and girls twirling and jigging, totally out of step, all around the organ-grinder. "Come on, let's dance!" says a teenager with a pockmarked face and a sad expression who seems to be the ringleader of the dancers. "We'll feel the cold less!"

"Right!" replies a freckle-faced girl who is dancing around him, dressed in an overcoat that is three sizes too big for her.

"But afterwards I'll be needing a beer to get me strength back."

"You'll get more than a pint of beer," says the pimply youth, gathering her into his arms and breaking into an apelike imitation of a waltz. "Pork stew . . . bacon and spuds . . . shrimps and little crabs . . ."

"Did you find a wallet in the street?" she inquires jokingly.

"Don't you worry none, sweetheart," replies the enterprising dancer. "I'll be satisfied with one of your sweet kisses in return."

"Over my dead body!" she says, shoving him away.

"You don't know what you're missing!" the young man replies, letting go of her and proceeding to put his arms around another girl who is dancing wildly not far away.

Andy watches the scene in amusement, but suddenly his mind is recalled, as if by orders from a higher power, to attend to the true purpose of his trip.

And so, saying good-bye to the bizarre group of dancers, he plunges back into the stinking, yellowish November fog, which stings his eyes, and goes on wandering through the narrow alleys until he comes upon a familiar-looking place.

Raising his eyes in the direction of a building, which reminds him of something, he is astounded to see the metal sign of the Jack-in-the-Box swinging from the side. The building isn't very different from the way he remembers it—the paint on the façade is peeling a bit less and the sign is a little less rusty.

When he goes in, he is even more surprised to see the long reception desk just as he remembers it. A child with thick, golden curls is sitting on the floor playing with a brightly painted wooden horse. When from behind the desk emerges a man with a limp and a long, droopy moustache who starts scolding the child, Andy can't help but identify William, "the Gimp," and his son, Sonny.

I wonder what kind of face Granddad Bob would make, Andy reflects, *if I told him that I'd met his father when he was a boy? One thing's for sure, he'd think I was out of my mind!*

When he first entered the Jack, he had felt somewhat reassured by the sight of so many familiar objects. "It's all so fantastic," he says aloud, certain that no one will hear him. "Pity nobody can see me."

And, in fact, they all go on ignoring him, including the little group of men who are sitting at a table next to the entrance playing whist and arguing animatedly. This foursome of customers, to judge from their appearance, don't seem to be doing all that well. Badly dressed in rather raggedy clothes, they don't smell too sweet either.

He approaches them to make a test and blows hard into the face of one of them who smells strongly of gin, just like Granddad Bob on certain occasions.

At once, the poor man begins waving his arm before his face as if trying to shoo away an insect. A second later he resumes talking at the top of his voice and playing his hand as if nothing has happened.

So Andy begins to stroll about again among the tables in the lobby. His eye falls on a crumpled newspaper lying on a table. It is a copy of the *Daily News* dated November 8, 1888.

This is crazy! he thinks a little uneasily. *I've travelled back in time.*

As William, dragging his game leg, goes on serving beer to the people sitting in the reception area, Andy decides to sit down near the group and listen to what they are saying.

"It's quite a while since we heard anything about Jack!" says the fattest of the three.

"Yes, it's been more than a month now and nary a word of him. The police haven't been able to do a thing. Just you wait and see, we'll never hear of him again."

"God knows where he's got to. At the very least, he's shipped out for somewhere and he's in Australia by now," adds the other.

"Knock it off, will you! Always talking about the same things," says the third man. "Isn't the doctor here this morning? He promised us a round of beers."

"Who . . . Tumblety?" William breaks in, overhearing them. "That drunken American went out early this morning and he hasn't come back yet and he's still got to pay me a week's rent! Word of honour . . . I'll have him by the scruff of the neck when he gets back; I'll show him who William Dobson is."

Andy listens to all this very carefully, thinking that everything he had heard about Grandfather William really was true.

What a character! He is rude to absolutely everybody!

Bored with sitting down, Andy wanders off behind the reception desk; seeing the big registration book open he decides to take a peek.

Dr. Tumblety is in room 5, the famous Mary Jane Kelly in room 4 and, in room 3, a certain Hippolyte Bollinger, a wine merchant. The other two names in the register mean nothing at all to him.

He takes Tumblety's room key, which is hanging behind him, and, since he had heard that the doctor was out, decides to take a stroll around the first floor.

He hurries up the stairs and arrives in front of the door of Tumblety's room without meeting anyone. The first thing he notices as he enters is a Gladstone bag with a very familiar look.

He recognises it right away, even though it is a little different from the way he remembers it from the day before—no!—more than a hundred and ten years later! The leather is shiny and without cracks, and the gold initials stamped on it glitter with a baneful gleam that to Andy seems at once to bode no good at all.

The room is very untidy: The bed is unmade and the desk is littered with a variety of small glass bottles that chemists use. When he opens the bag, he is surprised to see that it contains— beside the usual scalpels, some gauze, and a stethoscope—a large kitchen knife with a serrated blade.

Could the monster really have been Tumblety? thinks Andy, a little upset, hastily closing the bag. Suddenly hearing footsteps, he looks for a hiding place. A moment later he remembers that no one can see him anyway and he calms down.

A pretty, rather plump young woman with red hair enters the room. In her arms she carries a large basket with sheets and towels. Humming to herself, she sets about tidying the room.

After changing the sheets, she goes to the window to shake out the rug. Andy enjoys watching her as she works, totally unaware of his presence.

Just as the girl is busy at her chores, in comes William.

Seeing him, Andy feels more than a little uneasy, not least on account of the way the man is walking: slowly and noiselessly. *What does he want?* He is approaching the unfortunate girl from behind without making the slightest sound.

His eyes glitter with a strange light. A thousand thoughts crowd into Andy's mind. *Is great-great-grandfather William the murderer?*

A chill, cold as a knife blade, runs down Andy's spine as, petrified, he watches William draw near the young woman who goes on calmly with her work.

All at once, William is on her with one leap. Taking her from behind, he flings her unceremoniously onto the bed.

She's done for now, Andy thinks in terror. *He's going to strangle her and then dismember her body.*

When the pair of them burst out laughing, rolling on the bed, Andy leaves the room feeling like a fool.

Great-great-grandfather William is a right rogue, he thinks. *There I was thinking that he might be Jack!*

He feels very sorry for his great-great-grandmother Angela. He leaves the boarding house and spends the afternoon wandering about the East End. *It sure was a pretty run-down area*, he thinks.

Returning to the boardinghouse in the late afternoon, he is attracted by the sound of an argument coming from the kitchen. William, in his usual aggressive tone is yelling at a meek-looking woman. Andy tries to make out what they are saying, but the woman's voice is drowned out by William's shouts. He looks furious.

When the woman asks a question, which Andy doesn't catch, William, after shaking her awhile, slaps her on the face, knocking her to the floor.

He's a real animal, this William. I come from a line of people like this?

Very puzzled, Andy decides he has seen quite enough of his disreputable ancestor. Undoubtedly, the woman with the bloody face, who is now sobbing and trying to get up off the floor, must be Angela—Sonny's mother. As Granddad

Bob used to say, she was no beauty, but she had her head screwed on straight. Living with this man couldn't have been easy.

He walks along the corridors of the Jack, listening to his thoughts. The little boardinghouse isn't much different from the one he lives in, back in the present. The stuffed animals are there on the walls. They look a little less mangy, but they still seem on the point of pouncing on him. The rough wooden dining tables are in slightly better shape. For the first time in his life Andy sees a fire burning in the fireplace.

Of course! For years now we have had central heating at home.

The crackling flame is the only cheerful note in the place; all around, the rest looks familiarly sinister. Just one difference: The tiger skin that usually lies dozing by the fender of the fireplace is now hanging on the wall. Sonny, seated on a blanket near the fire, is playing with a wooden abacus.

Poor little kid! thinks Andy. *Always alone and with a father like that . . .*

He recalls that when he had entered Dr. Tumblety's room he had had a very strong sensation of cold. Chills had run down his spine as if he had perceived something frighteningly evil. He makes up his mind to keep an eye on that room.

When evening comes, after stealing something to eat from the kitchen, an art in which he is a professional, Andy throws himself down on the only sofa in the reception area. It is a gold-coloured velvet one with the springs poking out through the upholstery.

He wants to get a look at Dr. Tumblety, the mere sight of whose personal effects had caused him so much anguish. Arming himself with patience, he awaits the return of the boarders. The first to arrive is a big, stout man with a short reddish beard who makes for the first floor. Just like that, on a hunch, Andy thinks that he could not be Tumblety. He looks too sedate—one of those types who will tell you that happiness is "a nice dinner with my friends," if you should happen to ask.

Angela, who, at that moment emerges from the kitchen to set the table for supper, greets him cordially.

"Good evening, Mr. Bollinger!"

It must be Hippolyte Bollinger, the wine merchant in room three, thinks Andy.

A half hour later, a young woman comes in. She is about one metre seventy tall, not very elegant, but attractive all the same.

In Andy's opinion, she looks to be about twenty-five years old. Her ash-blond hair is gathered at the back of her neck in a bun and held by a long wooden pin. The sight of the red shawl she wears over her shoulders makes Andy jump, for he has suddenly remembered Massimo's story about young Mary Kelly.

As she enters the reception area with her companion, a small man with a provincial air who stinks of rotting fish, she laughs out loud. Still laughing, the pair of them go towards the stairs leading to the first floor.

Andy is struck by the simple beauty of the girl, who must be none other than Mary Jane Kelly, since he saw her take the key marked 4 from the hook.

It wasn't long before the two came back down to reception. The fishmonger says goodbye to Mary Jane, and she goes back upstairs.

Andy spends some hours in this manner, first sitting, then stretching out on the golden velvet divan. There is certainly a lot of coming and going at the Jack. The lodgers from the attic arrive too, a down-and-out poet and an Irish nursemaid.

Mary Jane has heaps of friends . . . How many times a day does she climb those stairs? Andy wonders after seeing her go up and down at least three or four times.

However, there is no sign of Dr. Tumblety. The key to room 5 still hangs in its place.

Angela is in the dining room snuffing out candles on the tables; Sonny has long been in bed; and William, drunk as usual, is shooting dice with his mates, swearing at them and especially at his luck, which is particularly bad this night. From time to time Angela passes through reception and casts worried glances at her husband.

She knows only too well how things will end: He will gamble and lose, he will get even drunker, and in the end he will take it out on her with a beating.

From time to time Andy dozes off on the sofa, only to be regularly awakened by the racket great-great-grandfather William and his friends make shouting out their bets over their game of craps.

It is 11:45 P.M. when Andy sees Mary Jane Kelly reenter the Jack, accompanied by a new client whose appearance is anything but reassuring. Badly dressed, his face is disfigured by the ravages of smallpox that he does his best to conceal behind a rather sparse ginger beard. He is cradling a crate of beer in his arms.

With all speed, Mary Jane and the man vanish to the upper floor.

He looks like a really ugly character, Andy says to himself. *Maybe he's the real Ripper.*

But about a half hour later, Andy hears heavy footsteps and sees the man with the pockmarked face coming down into the lobby, promptly disproving his hypothesis. He no longer holds the crate of beer.

A few minutes later, Andy's attention is grabbed by the sound of sweet singing coming from the floor above. Curious, he bounds up the stairs to the first floor and, following the sweet notes drifting on the air, finds himself a moment later standing before the door of room 4.

It was indeed Mary Kelly who was singing and her musical lament is not new to Andy. Recalling Massimo's story, he recognises the words of the song, "A Violet from My Mother's Grave."

So . . . this is the fateful night, Andy thinks.

Then, overcome by curiosity, he bends down and places his eye to the keyhole, to see what is happening inside the room. Mary Jane, wearing a long white nightgown, is pacing nervously up and down still singing. She has a bottle of beer in her hand and to judge from the rather strident way she is singing, it is not her first.

She's still alive, then!

Reassured, Andy returns to the ground floor and throws himself back down on the sofa. It is not yet two in the morning when he falls asleep lulled by "A Violet from My Mother's Grave," which Mary Jane Kelly shows no sign of stopping singing.

An unpleasant feeling of cold wakes Andy up. All the candles are out and there is nobody left in the room. He glances at the grandfather clock near the entrance.

Nearly four in the morning! And no singing anymore.

The only light that penetrates the room comes from the streetlamps shining through the entrance, illuminating the deserted hallway.

Andy sees that the fire in the dining room fireplace had gone out. A chill grips the room—and Andy. Without stopping to think, Andy runs to the key rack behind the reception desk.

Curses! The key to Tumblety's room is no longer in its place. So, the mysterious American doctor has come back in!

Trying to overcome his fear, Andy races up the stairs two at a time as if he is fleeing the darkness. He wishes he were somewhere else—anywhere but here. He says a silent prayer. If this were a dream, he would have wanted to wake up.

The first floor is silent and deserted, and there is even less light. Andy has to feel his way along, taking great care not to bump into one of the numerous little columns. A weak strip of light filters from under the door of Mary Jane Kelly's room, dimly illuminating the corridor.

Andy presses his ear to her door, but can hear nothing.

After he has moved to Dr. Tumblety's door and repeated the operation, his attention is caught by the noise of something passing by in the street. He goes to the window and catches a glimpse of a horse-drawn police van making its customary rounds. Suddenly, the sound of a door opening draws his attention and, at the same time, freezes the blood in his veins.

He whips around just in time to see a shadow turning the corner and heading for the stairs. He makes an attempt to follow the figure but finds that his legs won't obey him. He is unable to take a step. Paralysed with fear, all he can do is listen to the sound of the footsteps as they fade away.

Panic seizes him when he realises that the footsteps he heard moving away were not ordinary but sounded as if the person were dragging a leg . . . like a cripple!

It isn't Tumblety at all! he manages to think. *This is the sort of thing you never want to find out about your relatives.*

Now the door to Mary Jane's bedroom stands half open. Gathering up his last ounce of courage, Andy approaches the door. Centuries may go by, but Andy will never be able to forget the sight that lay before his eyes when he slowly opened the door of room 4. A candle set at the centre of the table in the modest room lights walls that appear to have been freshly painted—but with the blood of the unfortunate girl.

Blood drips copiously from her body and has already formed a fair-sized pool on the floor. The trunk, completely disembowelled, is at the centre of the bed, the intestines hanging out and trailing sadly down towards the floor like the branches of a weeping willow. The red shawl is still draped around her shoulders.

The wide-open, terrified eyes of the poor girl now staring blankly at Andy look sadly like one of those stuffed animals that decorates the walls in this house of horrors.

The only sound Andy can hear is his teeth chattering madly. He takes two steps back and, after standing still as if turned to stone for several seconds, starts racing down the corridor.

Back in the huge sitting room on the ground floor, after tripping over a carpet and cutting his knee badly on the fire poker, he dives to the floor behind the divan. Again paralysed with fear and bleeding from the knee, he waits for dawn. It is only when the first timid rays of sunlight begin to creep in from the street that Andy, hearing noise, finds both the courage and the strength to peep out from behind the divan where he had spent the longest night of his life.

Dozens of policemen crowd the reception area and are running up and down the stairs. A few minutes later, two men in white smocks come down the stairs carrying a sheet-draped body and disappear at once out of the entrance to the boardinghouse.

Poor thing! thinks Andy. *What a horrible end. Poor Mary Jane*!

One of the policemen, a man with a large handlebar moustache who seems to be the highest in rank, is standing in the centre of the room, questioning Angela and William. The latter, just for a change, is shouting.

Angela, her face drawn, twists her hands nervously and tries to calm him down, receiving only insults for her pains. The moustachioed policeman is asking them if one of their boarders is missing.

"That bloody American! He went off without even paying his bill!" says William. Andy can't make it out: Tumblety has run off from the hotel and William is still here. He glances at the key rack. The key to room 5 is now there, calmly hanging in its proper place, as if nothing had happened.

Andy approaches the group and peeps at the notebook in which the policeman is carefully writing his report: London, November 9, 1888, Jack-in-the-Box boarding house, 22 Batty Street, Mary Jane Kelly.

"Mr. Dobson," the policeman asks rudely "what did you do yesterday evening?"

"What the devil do you think I did?!" he shoots back. "We played our usual game of dice and we drank a few beers and then . . . and then off to dreamland. Then this morning I go to Mary Jane Kelly's room to demand the back rent— because the whore still owed me forty-five shillings—and I found her the way you saw her yourself. All carved up. Now who's going to give me my forty-five bob? And I'll have to spend more to have the room cleaned, with all that blood and guts spread all over the place. Damn it to hell!" William Dobson walks away, swearing, while the policeman with the handlebar moustache is scribbling everything down in his notebook.

Andy follows the questioning of two or three of the others present with great attention. Inspector Walter Beck—that is the name of the policeman with the outsized moustache—is carrying out the investigation in a very professional manner; but from his attitude you can tell that, personally, he doesn't hold out much hope of solving the case.

Jack, or whatever the devil his name is, has been thumbing his nose at the London Metropolitan Police for weeks now with his ghoulish letters, and so far there is no trace of him. All the suspects who have been detained had to be released since there was no evidence against them.

The interrogation that interests Andy the most involves a certain Mr. Hutchinson who says he saw Mary Jane wandering around in the area.

"I was coming back from Rumford about two in the morning and I ran into Mary Jane, standing under a lamppost, talking cheerfully enough to a man. They were laughing and joking. I got a real good look at him—he was right under the lamppost."

"Would you be able to describe him in detail?" asks Inspector Beck of Scotland Yard.

"Yes, yes," replies Hutchinson, full of zeal. "I looked at him well because he was a real gent, the sort you don't see much around these parts. Must have been someone with plenty of money, I thought. He was wearing a dark hat pulled down over his eyes. He had a dark complexion and a big moustache turned up at the ends and wore a long black coat with astrakhan trim, white collar and black tie, dark spats, and carried gloves. In other words a real gentleman! The thing that struck me most was a heavy gold chain across his waistcoat. It had a big seal with a red stone hanging from it, big enough to blind you, it was! I remember thinking he was one of the usual toffs looking for thrills . . . and then—?"

"That'll be all. You can go, Mr. Hutchinson." Inspector Beck cuts him short brusquely, snapping shut his notebook.

After the policemen have left, the group of curious onlookers begins to thin out too. In a couple of minutes the lobby of the Jack-in-the-Box is deserted. William and Angela go to the upper floor armed with scrubbing brushes and buckets;

evidently they are going to start ridding room 4 of its hellish bloodstains.

All that is left for Andy to do is to curl up on the sofa. *It all adds up—a straightforward affair*, thinks Andy.

He is so tired and shaken that he falls asleep straightaway.

XVI

Opening his eyes, Andy tries to put his hand to his aching head but finds that he can't. His right arm is tightly anchored to the chair in Massimo's room. One thing is sure, the Italian is good at tying knots! He feels as if a herd of buffalo is stampeding inside his skull.

It must be the result of that stuff he shot into me, Andy thinks. He gets up and staggers to the bathroom, dragging the armchair behind him. Not a sign of Massimo. *Where has he got to?*

He cuts the bindings tying him to the armchair with a pair of scissors and starts massaging the place where Massimo had inserted the needle. The only sign that remains of the injection is a tiny, nearly invisible purple mark.

"Thank God you're all right!" says Massimo who, at this very moment enters the room quite out of breath. "You had convulsions and you were mumbling gibberish. I nearly died of fright and I went upstairs to find Dr. Whitmore, but he wasn't there, so I came back here. I swear it's great to see you on your feet."

"I'm not sure I'm quite recovered yet," replies Andy in a slow, calm tone, as if he doesn't quite realise what has happened. "I can't even tell you what sort of experience it was. . . . It was extraordinary. . . . But now I ache all over and my head's going round . . . I'm chilled as if I'd spent a night in the open, and . . . I don't mind admitting, I'm a bit frightened. However, if you ask me if it was worth it, the answer is yes!"

"Well, thank goodness for that!" was all that Massimo, who now is a little more reassured, can say.

Andy begins to describe the experience he had and Massimo listens very closely. Andy tells him about the East End in 1888; about William and the chambermaid; about Tumblety, whom he hadn't even seen; about the previous night; and the horror he had felt when he entered poor Mary Jane's room. However, he mentions nothing about the chilling suspicion that had gripped him during his time in the past—the suspicion that Jack might be William, whose footsteps he had heard so distinctly right after the crime.

"But how long has it been?" Andy inquires, looking out of the window. "It's almost dark out there!"

"Nearly eight o'clock," replies Massimo. "You were unconscious for almost five hours."

"Wow," adds Andy with a smile, "to me it's like I've been away for a year. Anyway, it seemed like a whole day and a night. . . . It was absolutely fantastic!

"It's obvious that Dr. Tumblety was Jack— the morning after the crime he disappeared. However, great-great-grandfather William was no saint either . . . always dead drunk and violent. Poor Angela . . . God knows what she had to put up with on account of that beast!"

"All right, then," says Massimo. "All's well that ends well. It's been a very exciting day. Tomorrow we'll have time to talk again and size up the situation, but for now you'd better let your mum see you. She's probably looking for you. Lucy has come to visit with her dad and I think she's waiting for you in your room."

XVII

Following Massimo's advice to the letter, Andy rushes to his room after going to the kitchen to say hello to his mum, granddad, and, naturally, to Harry Catlett.

Lucy looks lovely. Burrowed into the armchair in Andy's room, engrossed in reading a book, she doesn't even notice his coming in. Very smartly dressed, she looks as if she came out of one of those fashionable boarding schools reserved for the upper classes—those schools where all the kids dress alike: low-heeled, patent-leather shoes, short blue velvet skirts with blouses the colour of mother-of-pearl with blue velvet collars and bows.

"Why did they dress you up like a box of chocolates?" Andy says interrupting her reading.

"They didn't dress me up, dummy! I've been dressing myself for quite a while now . . . But when we go visiting, Dad wants me to look smart and so . . . here I am. Your experiment . . . how did it go?"

For the second time in the space of just a few minutes, Andy recounts what he had experienced, sharing with her his suspicions concerning the identity of Jack the Ripper.

"You see what the essential question is? My great-great-grandfather might have been the murderer, and so I might be the descendant of a monster! I feel sick to my stomach when I think of it."

"Look, it was just a dream," she replies.

"Yeah, yeah. You make it sound easy. You're not the one who's the great-great-grandson of a monster."

"Relax, Andy. Would you like me to read you some of this?" Lucy continues, waving the book under his nose. "It's the book Massimo lent you with the letters that Jack the Ripper sent to the newspapers and the police; they're really quite horrifying."

"Forget it. I've already seen and heard enough nauseating stuff for one day."

But Lucy, who wants to get him back for his crack about her clothes, starts reading some passages from the letters contained in the book.

"This is the letter that starts 'Dear Boss', dated September 27, 1888, and sent to the Central News Agency. Initially it was thought to be a forgery but, following the murders of Eliazbeth Stride and Catherine Eddowes, the police were forced to reconsider, especially when they learned that the ears of one of the victims had been cut off, as had been promised in the letter. . . . Listen, I'll read it to you."

"Lucy, drop it!" Andy pleads. "I told you I'm not in the right mood. I'm feeling sick as it is . . ."

"Please . . . I'll just read a tiny bit—please!"

At this point, in the face of such persistence, all Andy can do is give up, and Lucy, all excited, starts to read some passages from Jack's letters.

"Dear Boss,
"I keep on hearing the police have caught me but they won't fix me just yet . . . I am down on whores and I shant quit ripping them till I do get buckled. Grand work the last job was. I gave the lady no time to squeal. How can they

catch me now. I love my work and want to start again. You will soon hear of me with my funny little games. I saved some of the proper red stuff in a ginger beer bottle over the last job to write with but it went thick like glue and I cant use it. Red ink is fit enough I hope ha. ha. The next job I do I shall clip the lady's ears off and send to the police officers just for jolly. . . . My knife's so nice and sharp I want to get to work right away if I get a chance. Good Luck.

Yours truly, Jack the Ripper"

The grey pallor of Andy's face does not bode well; he has evidently been exhausted by his extraordinary experience. He begins to rub his hands over his stomach and to swallow visibly while Lucy, still not satisfied, goes on reading, paying no attention.

"Listen to this. It's the letter Jack wrote when he sent a cardboard box containing part of a kidney of one of his victims, pickled in wine, to George Lusk, the president of the Whitechapel Vigilance Committee. This letter is nicknamed 'From hell'."

"Mr. Lusk . . . I send you half the Kidne I took from one women and prasarved it for you tother part I fried and ate . . . it was very nise. I may send you the bloody knif that took it out if you only wate a whil longer

    signed

    Catch me when you can Mishter Lusk"

"Don't you find it absolutely bloodcurdling?"

Lucy hasn't yet finished when Andy takes off like a rocket in the direction of the bathroom, clutching his belly with both hands. The sound of the toilet flushing leaves Lucy in no doubt as to what is going on.

Andy emerges from the bathroom soon after, his face a ghostly shade. "I told you I was feeling nauseated," he mumbles through clenched teeth. "I hope you're satisfied now."

"I'm sorry. If I had realised it was so serious . . ." she replies contritely. "Maybe you should get into bed now and have a good, long sleep."

Without a word Andy lets himself fall limply onto the bed, where he falls asleep almost instantly. All that remains for Lucy to do is to return to her father, who is waiting in the lobby.

Before leaving Andy, however, like a loving mum, she carefully removes his shoes and covers him well with an eiderdown.

Andy sleeps through the night, and in the morning finds himself already dressed and ready to go. A quick splash of water on his face and he's off into the street, braving the nippy morning air.

On the way to school he gives a more detailed account of the previous day's experiment to Lucy, who can still scarcely believe what he is saying. She by no means shares her friend's enthusiasm, and all the way to school, she begs Andy to abandon the dangerous game; but Andy refuses to listen to reason, even though, deep down inside, he has some misgivings of his own.

"You see, Lucy, the thing that bothers me most is the thought that, if my suspicions are right, I am *related* to a revolting creature. You should have seen the state that room was in. Still, it was a fantastic experience. I wish you could come with me next time," he says with a mocking grin.

"You can forget that for a start!" Lucy cuts him short, her cheeks redder than usual with anger. "I'm not fond enough of you to follow you in every mad adventure you get into. I can hardly believe you are reckless enough not to realise that all this is senseless. . . . Look at you, you even feel bad now thinking that one of your ancestors may have been a bloodthirsty maniac. When I think of it, I'm not all that sure I want to marry someone with such a monstrous family tree."

"Now I'm going to carve you up!" roars Andy, laughing at the same time. He raises his arms in the air like claws as if he were about to pounce on Lucy.

"You're a complete idiot!" she says, looking him up and down with an air of commiseration. "And anyway, you're not even funny."

They don't exchange another word the whole morning. When school is over and Andy invites her to tea, Lucy stops sulking and accepts readily enough.

XVIII

As they approach the little boardinghouse they are surprised to see an unusual amount of activity in front. Several police cars with flashing lights stand parked in the street; and a large, blue ambulance, its beacon flashing, is right in front of the door, its large rear door raised.

All around, a dozen or so policemen and at least the same number of men wearing white coats and rubber gloves are swarming like maddened bees.

Andy starts racing like a sprinter toward the entrance. A policeman grabs him, but Andy wriggles free like an eel and manages to enter the guest house, disappearing from Lucy's sight though she tries hard to keep up.

Shooting into the hall like a rocket, he sees his mum and granddad Bob talking to Lucy's dad and he heaves a sigh of relief.

"What's happened, then?" he asks.

He doesn't even wait for an answer; as Lucy joins him, he grabs her by the hand and hurries towards his room, dragging her with him.

The corridor leading to his room is crowded with uniformed policemen, too; when, soon after, they meet two bearers carrying a stretcher covered with a white sheet, they realise that something awful has once again happened at the Jack-in-the-Box.

Moving aside, they stand silent and still, watching the passing of that melancholy burden. Just as the stretcher is passing in front of them, one of the bearers stumbles. The stretcher jolts and from beneath the covering sheet a dark-skinned hand with elegantly varnished nails dangles limply.

The long, slim, ebony fingers are bedecked with gold jewelry that Andy knows very well—

"*Carla!*" he howls at the top of his voice, recognising that the victim is his friend the Jamaican woman.

Terrified, Andy simply cannot believe what he is seeing. Lucy, feeling faint, hugs him tight. Instinctively he puts his arms around her without even realising what he is doing (he is that shocked).

Two policemen are standing guard in front of the half-closed door to Carla Cooper's room; they pay no attention to the youngsters.

Before going into his own room, dragging a totally shocked Lucy behind him, Andy has time to glance into the poor woman's room. It is only a second, but it is long enough for him to glimpse a sight already familiar to him: the room has been turned upside down and blood is spattered nearly everywhere.

The two kids are joined in Andy's room some minutes later by Andy's mum, Lucy's dad, as well as Mr. Hugo Drabber. Neither Andy nor Lucy has spoken a word, so shocked are they. The stern frown on the face of Harry Catlett, member of the London Metropolitan Police, bears eloquent testimony to the heavy atmosphere of tension that fills the place.

"Lucy, I don't think this is the best place for you to be," he begins in a grave tone.

There is no reply. At that point Hugo Drabber, who also looks visibly shaken, says, "Poor child!

Don't be too hard on her. . . . I think she's scared enough as it is. Things like this never happen to us down in the country. It's a fact! You just can't live in the city anymore. I can't imagine a person having the courage to commit such an atrocity!"

Lucy's father, completely ignoring Drabber, goes on slowly and sternly. "Andy, I know that we have never gotten on all that well, but, leaving aside our differences for the moment, let's try to meet each other halfway, because, as you probably realise, the situation is extremely serious.

"Miss Cooper has been murdered in the room opposite yours, and I prefer to spare you the details. I know you're a smart kid and that nothing escapes you, so, if you have noticed anything that could be of use to us, please tell me about it."

Andy puts up his hands up in a gesture of surrender and says, "What can I say? The guilty party must be someone from the outside. . . . You yourself have seen the people who live here—they all look ordinary enough. There's Mr. Drabber," he says, pointing at him, "Dr. Whitmore . . . There's the Italian student who's here in London preparing his thesis and—"

"Ah, yes! that Italian student," Harry Catlett interrupts him. "He's not been a university student for a long time now. He got his degree three years ago, and so this thesis thing is just an excuse. I ran a check on him a few days back."

"What do you mean, he's not a student anymore?" Andy exclaims. He is starting to feel bewildered.

"I mean that, at the moment, this is the only certain information we have on him; but soon I should be getting his file from Italy. At that point our Signor Massimo, or whatever his name is, will have no more secrets. But you look a bit upset by this. Is there something you know and don't want to tell me?"

"I've got nothing to tell you. . . . Wouldn't it be quicker just to ask *him*?" says Andy, shrugging his shoulders yet unable fully to conceal his surprise.

"I'd ask him if I could find him," says Lucy's dad. "We're looking for him, but he seems to have disappeared."

"Uh . . . um . . . when did the crime take place? This morning?" Andy asks, pointing a finger in the direction of Carla Cooper's room.

"The coroner tells us that Miss Cooper was murdered about twenty-four hours ago."

An ice-cold chill runs the length of Andy's body.

Massimo is not a student! he thinks. *And when I recovered consciousness yesterday he wasn't in the room and the murder was committed yesterday afternoon . . . and then . . . all that interest in the 1888 murders . . . what for, if he isn't a student?"*

Almost as if he were rising from a sea of thoughts in which he was immersed, Andy repeats that he has nothing more to say.

"Well, however it is," says the policeman, "we'll be keeping an eye on this Massimo fellow; and if he knows something or if he's involved in this I swear I'll make him sweat blood, the damned dope addict! Ah, yes. I am forgetting . . . we found a syringe in his room, hidden in a case."

"Oh, really?" says Andy, pretending to be surprised.

"In any case," Lucy's dad concludes, "I'm off now, but I'll leave one of my men in the hotel to watch over your mum and make sure she comes to no harm."

After Henry Catlett leaves taking Lucy with him, all the others follow him out of the room, including Andy's mum, who wanders out without a word.

It is by now nearly three in the afternoon, and Andy throws himself on his bed and begins to reflect on what is going on.

Carla . . . he sobs, holding his reggae CD to his chest.

After a short time, overcome by an enormous tugging at his tonsils, he dozes off.

XIX

The following day a strange atmosphere lies over the Jack-in-the-Box. Andy tries to persuade himself that nothing can happen that would be more tragic than what has already taken place. So why is he filled with a feeling of impending disaster?

Accompanied by these ominous thoughts he goes to school, where, throughout the morning, his schoolmates besiege him with questions concerning Carla's murder.

He is very sparing with the details: He doesn't feel like telling stories about his family. Lucy is under strict orders from her father not to visit Andy's house. This makes them both very unhappy, but they promise to phone each other. Coming home from school as hungry as a wolf, Andy shoots into the dining room like a guided missile.

Emma, frowning and tight-lipped, is very busy serving a late lunch to the guests. Everyone is present. Next to Granddad Bob, Hugo Drabber is paying his respects, as usual, to the roast beef by stuffing himself with it, while Dr. Whitmore is engaged in one of his usual learned dissertations about some problem connected with his chemical experiments.

What sort of people are they? Andy thinks, *They carry on as though nothing has happened.*

Massimo is there, too, sitting a little apart. Scotland Yard had questioned him the whole morning, and he appears to have succeeded in convincing them that he had nothing to do with the murder.

At another table sits Harry Catlett with a fellow constable, who has been left on duty at the Jack.

After gazing sadly for some moments at the empty chair usually occupied by Carla Cooper, Andy speaks to Massimo with an air of provocation. "How are your studies coming along?"

"I can explain . . ." He is clearly embarrassed and invites Andy to his room that afternoon. Andy doesn't even bother to reply. He sits down and, with his head bent, eats his meal without speaking a word to anyone. An hour later, in

Massimo's room, the two take up the discussion once more. To judge from the two large open suitcases filled with books and clothes which lie on the bed, Massimo is about to leave.

"Andy, I quite understand that you're mad at me, and I can't blame you. But if I lied it was only so I would be able to continue with my work.

"It's true! I'm not a university student. I'm a newspaper reporter, and, since people in my profession aren't very well liked, I made up a story because I was afraid you wouldn't help me.

"You see, I'm writing a series of articles about great unsolved mysteries, and the Jack-in-the-Box seemed like a good starting point. Then I met you . . . but I didn't mean to make a fool of you. Quite to the contrary, I like you a lot and . . . I know I'll miss you."

"You might have told me you were a journalist," replies Andy, whose anger is beginning to fade. "It wouldn't have changed anything. I'd have been glad to help you."

"It doesn't matter very much now," says Massimo as he places some more things in the suitcase with a disconsolate air. "I'm going back to Italy. My boss has called me home; he says that in two months I haven't achieved anything and that he's tired of throwing his money down the drain."

"But . . . what about what happened to me! What we did together. The injection . . . my dream—all wasted?"

"What do you expect me to do, Andy," he says lighting a cigarette, "go to my chief and tell him that a boy I met has strange powers and that, after I gave him an injection, he went into a trance and travelled more than a century back in time?

"At the very least I'd be fired and then they'd have me put in a lunatic asylum. No, no! It's all over. I've got a flight booked for Italy tomorrow afternoon. I only hope that you're not too mad at me."

"No," Andy says, "I understand now. And to think that for a second, when they told me that you weren't a student, I thought it might have been you who killed Carla—seeing how she was murdered during the time I was unconscious and, when I woke up, you weren't there in your room."

"So much for the faith you have in me!" Massimo says, breaking into a laugh. "Can you imagine *me* chopping people into bits? It's absolutely absurd!"

"Yeah . . . when I think about it now . . . but before! How was I to know? All you did was lie."

"And your special gift, doesn't it tell you anything about this affair?" asks Massimo gently.

"It's a kind of special situation. I feel very confused. This thing is making me very nervous since I'm personally involved. Apart from that, it's very different from the other times. I mean, there's a big difference between guessing what's inside a drawer to amuse and surprise your friends and trying to see clearly a situation like this. . . . But I *am* worried. At certain times it's as if I can feel evil materialising within the decaying walls of this place, but I can't really get it into focus."

Massimo, standing in the centre of the room, gives a last look around almost as if he wants to impress it on his memory so he will never forget it. "I'm going to miss these musty walls . . . and your mum's roast, too. She's a dear woman; take care of her and protect her."

"You can count on that," replies Andy with a touch of pride. "Ah! I must give you back your

CD, the Niccolò Paganini one. . . . I really enjoyed it. I closed my eyes while I was listening, and went into a daydream . . . it brought me a lot of peace. That Paganini must have been quite something, and the Stradivarius violin really rocks. . . ."

"Consider it a present from me."

"I have the feeling we'll meet again someday, Massimo," Andy says, trying to play down a farewell scene that is becoming a little too sentimental. "And if I feel it, you can bet it will happen."

"I sure hope so," Massimo whispers giving Andy a big hug.

CHAPTER

XX

Later on, while Andy is in his room thinking over
what has happened, someone knocks at the door.
It is Mr. Hugo Drabber.

He enters, carrying a bulky package wrapped
in newspaper that he deposits on Andy's bed.
"I'm sure you've never seen one made like this!"
he says, unwrapping the parcel and taking out a
tangle of string and wooden sticks.

It was all the material needed to make a kite;
kites are Hugo Drabber's lifetime passion.

"This is my gift to you. All you have to do is
assemble it—a spot of glue, a few knots—and
then off you go running through the fields!"

In Andy's view, kites are idiotic and the people
who run with them are even more so. Without
much enthusiasm, he thanks Drabber anyway.
Considering what is going on at the Jack, it doesn't

seem to him that this is the most appropriate moment for pastimes of this kind.

"And, besides, to encourage you, I'll promise you five quid if you manage to assemble it by tomorrow morning! Do you want to bet?"

When Hugo had gone, Andy thinks it over for a bit; he doesn't care a hoot about the kite, but the promise of five pounds makes the project quite interesting.

He decides he will set to work after supper. Right now, the top priority is his afternoon phone call to Lucy.

"I'm sorry your dad won't let you come here. Mr. Drabber gave me a kite."

"Be careful, Andy. He seems a bit touched to me. . . ."

"You're joking! He's an absolutely charming person. He's only got one fault: gluttony. According to Mum, he's got an appetite like a wolf—she says she wants to charge him extra board on account of the way he stuffs himself."

"This evening, stay in your room and please don't get it into your head to go snooping around somewhere." Lucy is looking for reassurance.

"What is it? Are you starting to worry?"

"Yes! You're so silly! It's about time you stopped poking your nose into things that happened over a hundred years ago."

"Relax, Lucy, everyone here is too taken up with worrying about the present to bother about the past. Besides, it's easy for you to talk. It's not you who might have an ancestor who was totally out of his mind—it's me! Think if they found out at school. First they'd start making fun of me, then they'd steer clear of me. In no time at all, I'd wind up begging on street corners."

"You're exaggerating as usual, and anyhow, you're not even sure!"

"What do you mean, I'm not sure. I heard someone limping that night . . . and then I saw what a nasty personality great-great-grandfather William had. I wouldn't be at all surprised if my suspicions turn out to be true."

"What night are you talking about, Andy? Massimo injected some kind of junk into you, and you dreamt it, that's all. . . ."

"So that's what you think? It was all a dream? When we meet tomorrow, I'll show you something and you'll change your tune. Just wait and see."

"Andy, I've got to run! If Mum catches me on the phone again I'm in trouble! Last month the bill was very high!"

"But I called you."

"Yes, Andy, but she'd never believe that. Everyone knows that you Dobsons are a stingy lot!"

"Yeah. 'Bye, then!"

"Bye-bye, kisses . . ." The rest of the evening passes fairly tediously. A dense, insistent drizzle has started falling over London, making the atmosphere even more oppressive and sombre.

This city is one enormous shower, Andy finds himself reflecting. *It'd be nice if the rain could wash away all the ugly things that are happening these days.*

He ends up doing nothing but brood over poor Carla's murder, the truly staggering experiment, and the suspicion that troubles him the most—his heritage. Is it really true that he is descended from an infamous murderer?

Right after supper and after giving Lucy a ring just to say hello, Andy gets down to the task of assembling the kite.

He begins organising the parts rather carelessly because the only thing that interests him are those blessed five pounds. . . .

With the money he would be able to buy some candy and crisps and treat Lucy to an ice cream in the West End. They would take the Underground on Saturday afternoon, then they would do some window-shopping and, on the way back, she would lean her head on his shoulder and fall asleep.

XXI

Kites! he thinks scornfully, *a pastime for dimwits! And this one's a really lousy-looking one. Just look at that shape!*

As he spreads out a large piece of flimsy dark paper on the bed, he gets a surprise. "Well what do you know!" Andy says out loud. "This thing is shaped like a bat! There it is—complete with raggedy wings and everything in place."

As he stares, grinning at the huge paper monster he can't help thinking that Mr. Drabber must be a very funny sort. *Hovering kites, my foot!* Andy thinks. *We've got a hovering bat here! I wonder why they call them kites in the first place?*

He fiddles about for quite some time with the strange gadget which, to him, seems at least as strange as the person who has given it to him. In the end, after assembling all the interlocking pieces, he discovers that he needs some glue.

As often happens, just when you need something it is nowhere to be found. He turns his room upside down before giving up and deciding to go and ask his mum, who always knows where everything is.

He hurries along the corridor to the kitchen, where he finds Granddad also engaged in a completely different type of search, cursing as he goes.

"Dammit! How is it you can never find anything in this house?"

"If you're looking for the gin," says Andy, surprising him, "you won't find it. Mum has moved it again. She must have noticed that you discovered the new hiding place.

"By the way, where is Mum? I need the pot of glue."

"To glue your mouth shut, I suppose," Granddad retorts sarcastically. Having said this, he decides to forget about the gin and make do with a beer. "Your mum must have gone to bring some chamomile tea to Hugo Drabber . . . seems he's got a terrible bellyache—indigestion more than likely!"

"He probably ate all the roast beef again."
Andy laughs. "I've always wondered where he
puts it all. Well, so much the worse for him."

His hunt for the pot of glue leads him straight
to the first floor; following the trail of his mum,
he then finds himself directly facing Hugo
Drabber's door.

Entering the room after knocking, he finds
Mr. Drabber wearing a fine, arabesque dressing
gown and holding an enormous pair of scissors
of the type that drapers use to cut off lengths of
cloth.

"Mr. Drabber, have you seen Mum by any
chance?"

"No, no, my boy! Not at all!"

"Ah!" says Andy. " It doesn't matter. But what
are you doing with those scissors? Gosh! I never
saw a pair that big, honest."

"Ehem . . . ah . . . in this weather it would be
sheer madness to go out . . . and anyway I haven't
even got an umbrella. So, I'm designing a new
kite. I'm a staunch proponent of the importance
of kites in the education of the individual.
Everyone ought to make kites!"

Andy nods with a wan smile but, inside, he feels that these sentiments are very odd indeed and that Mr. Drabber is more than a little bit odd.

"By the way, how is yours coming along?" the old country gentleman asks.

"Ah, the big bat? Fine, fine, get ready to hand over five pounds. And your tummy ache . . . how is it?"

"Eh?" says Drabber putting his hand on his paunch as though he has suddenly remembered that he has one. "Oh . . . yes, er . . . much better, thank you."

"Well, I'll be off, then."

"Wait, Andy. Since you're here, my breakfast tray has been here since this morning. You don't mind, do you?" says Drabber, pointing to the tray with his large finger.

You sure have to be awful polite for five quid! Andy thinks as he makes his way downstairs carrying the tray with a teacup on it. He has almost reached the kitchen when he is assailed by "the hotsies." He knows them very well. Every time his strange powers begin to kick in, he is seized by a sensation of suffocating heat that Lucy jokingly calls "the hotsies."

And, as certain as anything, every time he is overcome by the sensation it means: *danger ahead!*

What the devil is going on! he thinks, wiping away the sweat that has started pouring down his forehead.

When he sniffs the empty teacup and smells chamomile flowers, his stomach balls itself up like a wad of paper and his heart leaps into his throat.

What an idiot!

Dropping the tray and cup, which breaks into smithereens, he sets off running in the direction of the dining room.

The young policeman, Mark Scampers, whose job it is to watch over the safety of the inhabitants of the hotel, is sprawled on the divan like a deflated set of bag pipes, watching TV.

Judging by his gaze, not exactly glowing with intelligence, it might have been any sort of programme; he wouldn't have noticed anyway. He is happy enough just to stare at the screen. In fact, Mark Scampers—that *is* his name—had managed to get into the London Metropolitan Police by pulling strings. His IQ was decidedly lower than average and, poor chap, he had never known either his dad or his mum. He is the kind of man you just can't help but feel a little sorry for.

Andy excitedly asks the policeman to follow him and a few seconds later, they are standing in front of Hugo Drabber's door.

"Empty!" yells Andy, kicking a chair in a fit of temper.

After a few moments of agonised hesitation, the two of them leave the room. An irresistible force draws Andy toward the door of room 4.

When, at Andy's panicked urging, Mark Scampers, who has not yet realised what is going on, breaks in the door with his shoulder, the scene that presents itself is very far from reassuring.

In the centre of the room, dimly lit only by the glow of a candelabra, sits Emma. She is tied tightly hand and foot to an old sturdy armchair.

A muffled moan of terror is all that comes from her mouth that is covered with duct tape.

Her wide staring eyes beg for help.

Standing motionless beside her is Hugo Drabber. He stares at the two newcomers. Only mindless folly can be read in his insane eyes.

He has the enormous pair of shears in his left hand, the points of the blades held threateningly to the throat of Andy's mum.

The whole scene is reminiscent of Hell.

The wavering light of the candles casts flickering shadows on the faces of all present as if they are surrounded by a crowd of cheering zombies waiting impatiently to take part in some bloody ritual.

Andy and the policeman stare petrified.

"Drop those scissors and get away from that chair!" orders P.C. Scampers in a trembling and most unconvincing tone.

"Having found me out will bring you no good, my friends!" thunders Hugo Drabber. "You will meet the same fate that I have reserved for this cursed woman. You are helpless against me, for you are vermin and I am . . . *Jack*!"

"What do you mean . . . Jack? Jack who? What are you talking about?" Andy hazards in an attempt to gain time and to distract him.

"My dear boy, your childish tricks and traps are not going to save her. She'll wind up just like that other one. She doesn't like kites either. I asked her and she just laughed. She laughed and laughed. She mocked me. . . ."

"Who did you ask . . . why did she laugh . . . *who*?" continues Andy desperately. He is already beginning to run out of subjects. . . .

"That friend of yours—that blasted air hostess." Drabber says in grim, menacing tones. "I brought her a kite, but she started to mock me . . . And then . . ."

"And then . . ." Andy inquires somewhat timidly, as if he were afraid to hear the answer.

"And then she threw me out of her room . . . still with that smirk on her face . . . All those white teeth . . . But in the end she stopped laughing at me . . . Jack's shining knife took her by surprise. It goes in through the throat and out through the back of the neck . . . I lift her up. Jack holds her fate in the palm of his hand. She's not laughing anymore, because you don't laugh at Jack the way you laugh at Hugo!

"And now," he adds, addressing Andy, "I've got the same fate in store for your mother."

Andy whispers to the young policeman who is standing beside him with no idea of what to do, "For God's sake, do something! This guy's going to kill my mum! You've got a gun haven't you?"

"Roger," mutters P.C. Scampers. But his tone lacks the slightest trace of conviction.

"I'm telling you for the last time—" the policeman finally decides to shout, taking a revolver from his jacket pocket— "drop those scissors and move back!"

As he speaks, he takes two or three paces toward Drabber, his arm extended, aiming the revolver.

All of a sudden, a large meat cleaver appears in Mr. Drabber's right hand which, until that moment, he had been concealing behind his back. His insane eyes, already wide open, dilate still further. In the feeble light of the candles, they give him the look of a tiger about to emerge from the darkness to lunge at its prey. . . .

A lightning-fast movement.

With the sinister glint of steel, the broad blade slashes through the air. A heart-rending howl of agony is torn from the throat of the young policeman: his hand, still gripping the revolver, lies on the floor, sliced completely off.

A jet of vermilion blood spurts copiously from the stump.

At the sight of this, Mark Scampers falls to the floor in shock. Drabber, laughing maniacally, bends over him, turning his back on Andy who can't believe his eyes.

After a couple of violent, hacking blows to the neck of the unfortunate policeman, the crazed Mr. Drabber straightens up.

Now staring straight at Andy, he raises his left hand in the air. Still brandishing the meat cleaver threateningly in his right hand, he begins to bear down on Andy with slow steps.

"Nobody is getting out of this room alive. . . . This is the return of Jack! . . . My triumph . . . my *masterpiece*!"

His face was now unrecognisable—totally transfigured—and his eyes are aflame with . . . *joy*.

"Now I am going to cut you up into tiny little pieces, you stupid boy! Then when I'm through with your mother, I'll be out of here. . . . I do hope you won't mind if I borrow one of your umbrellas—the weather's foul and, in any case, you'll certainly won't be needing it."

He's mad as a hatter, thinks Andy, incredulous.

An instant later a sound like thunder, followed by a flash like a bolt of lightning shakes the room.

Something that looks like a red rosebud appears on Hugo Drabber's neck. He drops to the floor like an empty sack, without a word or even a whimper.

All Andy can do is stand immobilised for a few seconds, staring at the scene as he grips the still-smoking police revolver in both hands.

He feels like puking he is so disgusted, but he holds it back. Throwing the revolver to the floor, he rushes to his mum, who has been staring horrified at the tragic scene, and he frees her from the armchair.

At that second, attracted by the report of the gun, Granddad Bob bursts into the room followed by Dr. Whitmore.

Though he had served in Africa during WWII, and therefore had already seen his share of dead bodies, old Bob finds it hard to control his panic. His hands are shaking uncontrollably.

The scene that presents itself to him is unbelievably gruesome. The body of the unfortunate policeman lies on the floor with his severed head resting in a dimly lit corner. A little further away,

Hugo Drabber, stretched out on the floor, is gasping and rolling in his own blood that is jetting frighteningly from the wound on his neck.

"Everybody out!" Granddad Bob orders in a shaking voice.

XXII

It is nearly three in the morning and the dreary drizzle seems to have no intention of letting up.

Through the windows, the flashing lights of the numerous police cars that had rushed to the front of the Jack sweep intermittently across the ground floor rooms, lighting up the people sitting in the dining room, giving their faces a surreal look.

All around, policemen, doctors, and nurses scurry back and forth.

Harry Catlett is more concerned about Emma's state of mind—she is in deep shock—than he is about collecting evidence.

"They've just called me from the hospital," says Lucy's dad in a steady, serious voice. "Hugo Drabber is going to live. But for the rest of his life he'll be making kites in the exercise yard of a prison for the criminally insane."

"Fine," replies Andy. "thinking of everything he did, death would be too easy on him."

"It's been a terrible night for the police," Mr. Catlett reminds them all. "We've lost one of our men." However . . . Andy . . . you did a great job."

"Thank you Mr. Catlett!" responds Andy with barely concealed pride. It is the first time Lucy's dad has ever said anything to commend him.

XXIII

Some weeks have passed since that infernal night, and Andy's mum has recovered fairly well from the shock and the trauma.

Both she and Grandfather Bob have gone back to their respective occupations. They act as if nothing has happened and do their best to behave as naturally as possible. But the harder they try, the more awkward and unnatural they look. They were like this for a while longer, but then everything went back to normal.

Time, as you know, sets all things right.

Andy, on the contrary, makes no effort at all to hide his state of mind. Quite apart from the shock of what has happened, he has to live with the horrible doubt that gnaws at him and which he can confide only to Lucy: Is he really the descendant of the bloodthirsty, demented Jack the Ripper?

Sometimes he even thinks he can hear the halting footsteps, the dragging foot that, ever since that night in 1888, haunts him like a bad dream. The torment of his uncertainty makes him surly and morose.

On the other hand, for the Dobson family, business is booming.

After what had happened, the Jack-in-the-Box has become an even more famous place. It is now even included in the tourist guides that had gone so far as to create a "Ripper Walking Tour" around Whitechapel and the other scenes of the 1888 crimes. It terminates right at the Jack-in-the-Box, where drinks and food are available to all. It's a grisly enough idea, to tell the truth, but an effective one because it tickles the curiosity of thrill-seeking tourists.

Lots of visitors passing through London ask if they can spend the night there, but, on account of the limited number of rooms, Emma has to refuse dozens of bookings every day.

The bar, run by Granddad Bob, is now a great success. If things go on like this, they will soon have enough money to do up the place and maybe even add on a couple of rooms.

What's more, Granddad Bob feels it is almost too good to be true that he is able to regale the tourists with his bloody tales—which he often makes up on the spot—without being scolded by Emma.

At first, Andy's mum was rather put out by all the commotion that had been created around her little boardinghouse; but then she had to admit that business is decidedly better and that, with the money, she will be able to ensure a good education for her son.

Massimo phones often from Italy.

Thanks to what happened, he managed to go back to Italy with a sensational scoop. With Andy's collaboration, he had succeeded in publishing several articles on the subject of the old and "new" Jack the Ripper story. His editor, recognising his merits, had even offered him a permanent position as a foreign correspondent.

In a taxi from London Airport, Massimo is thinking once again about the whole affair and how blind chance can sometimes allow one to witness the most unbelievable events.

He was delighted to have accepted an invitation from Andy and his family to attend a party to celebrate their narrow escape from danger and the improvement of their business.

The dining room, freshly painted and covered with festive decorations, is nearly unrecognisable. The worn, rough wooden tables are covered with red tablecloths, and on each table stand solid silver three-branched candelabras that cast a warm, reassuring glow over the whole room.

Even the tiger skin, in its place in front of the fireplace—which on this joyful occasion is crackling cheerfully—looks more reassured.

When Massimo enters the dining room, Andy and Granddad Bob are setting the tables with huge trays weighed down with appetising sandwiches and savouries.

"Is this the Hotel of the Monsters?" Massimo says loudly to attract their attention.

After a warm hug, Andy and Massimo sit down at a table. Lucy joins them. For the occasion, she is wearing a lovely red dress with patent leather shoes. Over a sandwich and glass of beer, Andy recounts the latest developments.

"Hugo Drabber has been locked up in a lunatic asylum after confessing to the murder of Carla Cooper and that poor policeman. I reckon he'll spend the rest of his life making kites that he'll never fly."

"Yes, yes, I know the whole story," says Massimo. "He had already killed two women before he came to London—he's a raving lunatic who thinks he is a descendant of Dr. Tumblety and that it was his duty to carry on his work."

"What a stupid idea!" says Andy glumly. "They probably weren't even related. . . . Maybe Tumblety wasn't Jack the Ripper at all," he adds, thinking back to his night in 1888 and of his suspicions about William, "the Gimp."

"No, no," Massimo interrupts, "it's practically beyond doubt now that Dr. Tumblety *was* Jack the Ripper. The only difference is that Mr. Drabber will rot in the madhouse while that cripple Tumblety got clean away in spite of the horrible crimes he was guilty of."

Andy and Lucy stare at each other, wide-eyed.

"Cripple? What do you mean, cripple?" demands Lucy with barely concealed amazement.

"It's not a well-known detail," Massimo reveals. Not knowing how much relief he is about to give Andy—and Lucy—he continues, "Tumblety had been lamed several years before in a bad fall from a horse. It's one of the facts I checked up on when I was going through papers at Scotland Yard; nobody ever talks about it because it's not considered to be important."

"Like fun, it's not important!" Andy exclaims, smiling.

"It sure is important!" echoes Lucy.

"Hey, kids, you're looking a bit weird!" Massimo replies, surprised at their reaction. "I think you'd better lay off the beer."

Before the arrival of all his schoolmates—at least a dozen of them—Andy, taking advantage of the fact that Massimo is occupied talking to his mum, takes Lucy by the hand and drags her off to his room.

"So, I'm *not* descended from a bloodthirsty monster," he says excitedly.

"Well! So much the better, don't you think?" Lucy says, teasing him. "You must swear from now on never to breathe a word to anyone about serial killers, dismembered bodies, and risky experiments. Who knows what sort of junk your friend Massimo injected into you to make you imagine all those things you think you experienced. You could have been left a drooling imbecile! And then—"

"And then again," Andy cuts her off, "it would be nice to think that it *was* all a dream, but I can't."

"What do you mean, you can't! You don't believe you really travelled through time, do you?" Lucy shouts in a fury.

"But there's something else. . . . I never told you so as not to scare you. Do you remember, when I was describing my journey into the past, that I told you I had cut myself on the fire poker while I was chasing after the footsteps of the mysterious cripple? Good! Okay, then, look here."

As he says this, he rolls the leg of his baggy jeans up above his knee to reveal an unmistakable, ugly scar.

"This is a souvenir of that night in 1888. What have you got to say now? You think I dreamed up this scar as well?"

"I say that if this is another of your usual jokes, it's not funny at all!" Lucy replies, perturbed.

"That's something we may never know." Andy says with a diabolical grin. Hugging her close as he has never done before in his life, he plants a great big kiss on her forehead.

Arm in arm, they walk along the corridor on their way to the dining room where the festivities are about to begin. It seems to Andy that the stuffed animal heads that decorate the walls are winking knowingly at him.

That afternoon goes by in a whirl of dancing and drinking.

The beer is provided free, so the whole neighbourhood, along with a crowd of nosy parkers, comes as if on a pilgrimage to the Jack-in-the-Box.

Andy is delighted to have discovered that he is not the offspring of an infamous monster, and he spends the afternoon in the company of his schoolmates, Massimo, and, of course, Lucy.

He is truly happy to see that his mum is at last serene, and he watches her as she dances with Lucy's Dad.

They would make a fine pair, he thinks, going a bit soft for the gruff policeman.

When one is happy, time flies.

The guests are thinning out, leaving behind mounds of empty glasses and bottles; and a plane is will take Massimo back to Milan that evening.

"Before I go there's one more thing I want to tell you. My publisher asked me to invite you over to Italy to thank you for what you did for us. He can set up a series of interviews and maybe a TV appearance. At the same time you could have a holiday. Naturally, it would all be paid for by my publisher. So . . . what do you think?"

The excitement and the joy of this news leaves Andy rooted to the spot for several seconds. Then, an instant later, as if he had been stung by a scorpion, he starts skipping about all over the room, yelling out his happiness like a madman to the astonishment of all.

"The boy is absolutely crazy. . . . He'll give me a load of problems, I just know it," Emma says, turning to Massimo with an air of resignation.

"The boy is a *phenomenon*, Mrs. Dobson. You're going to be very proud of him, because one day soon he's going to *be* somebody," replies the Italian with a look that astounds her.

"It's true!" adds Granddad Bob, his eyes turning misty. "We Dobsons are a special sort of folk."

A NOTE TO THE READER

The events of the 1888 Jack the Ripper murders depicted in this book accurately follow the historical records of the case. Given the nature of fiction, however, one important fact has been altered. Mary Jane Kelly was not murdered at 22 Batty Street. She actually lived in a room known as No. 13 Miller's Court, at 26 Dorset Street, a short distance from 35 Hanbury Street, where Mary Ann Nicholls was murdered.

CLAUDIO APONE

A NOTE ON THE TYPE

The text was set in 11 point Bauer Bodoni with a leading of 15 points space. In 1926, under the direction of Heinrich Jost, Louis Höll cut the punches for the Bauer typefoundry's version of Bodoni. Bauer Bodoni is closest to the original Bodoni in its proportions and characteristic refinement and delicacy. Bodoni was designed by and named after the prolific Giambattista Bodoni of Parma, Italy, who designed his famous types at the end of the eighteenth century. Bodoni is one of the signifiers of the modern style of type design, with its dramatic difference in thick and thin letter strokes, severe vertical stress, and extremely fine, delicate serifs and hairlines.

⌐

The text display font is Copperplate Gothic, designed by Frederic W. Goudy in the early 1900s for American Type Founders. Copperplate Gothic appears at first to be a sans serif, but actually has very small, fine serifs. Copperplate Gothic is used in many varieties of commercial printing, business cards, and lettering on the frosted-glass office doors of lawyers and private investigators.

Composed by Charles B. Hames
New York, New York

Printed and bound by
Maple-Vail